BEFORE THE ASTEROIDS

By
HARL VINCENT

I0616906

ARMCHAIR FICTION
PO Box 4369, Medford, Oregon 97504

For more information about Armchair Books and products, visit our website at…

www.armchairfiction.com

Or email us at…

armchairfiction@yahoo.com

THIS PLANET WAS DOOMED!

Of the unexplained mysteries of our solar system, none present more possibilities for the imagination than the origin and nature of the asteroids—ranging in diameter from a few miles to several hundred. These bodies seem to present an eternal question mark to the scientists endeavoring to discover how our system came into existence.

Harl Vincent's ingenious story recounts a stirring interplanetary drama. Vincent supposes that a tremendous conflict to the death may have been waged between highly civilized races. Long has it been that war has torn families and neighbors apart; in this classic tale, war seeds the destruction of an entire planet—possibly explaining what was there Before the Asteroids…

FOR A COMPLETE SECOND NOVEL, TURN TO PAGE 93

CAST OF CHARACTERS

RONAL
More than just a handsome prince, he was a strong leader who brought his people honor…and saved them from certain doom.

ILA
This beautiful princess, beloved by all who met her, disowned her father…and denounced her planet as depraved.

TORVEG XI
Under this wise and much respected monarch, the metropolis of Marida had enjoyed its happiest and most peaceful era.

ANDITES
An academician who had powerful insight into the fate of his world…though his monarch thought he was just an alarmist.

OLAR
This vile creature was the cruel dictator of the planet Voris, unafraid to slay even his closest allies and family. .

MIRSA
Olar had a strange obsession for this beautiful young woman of Arin—an obsession she used to save her world.

ANDON
A brilliant engineer who knew the spaceships of Voris inside and out. His defection could prove vital to the survival of Arin.

FOREWORD

MORE than a half million earth years have passed since Olar, son of Nur, ruled supreme in the land of Keron. He was the last of a long line of despots; and, likewise, last of the rulers of the great empire that dominated the planet Voris.

In those days there were but two inhabited bodies in the solar system; the other being Arin, now known to us as Mars, and considerably younger in its civilization than was Voris, whose orbit lay between those of Mars and Jupiter. The two planets were quite similar in physical characteristics; though their seasons were somewhat different because of the greater inclination of the equator of Voris to its orbit; its faster rotation, and its longer period of revolution. But the peoples were so alike in appearance that they could scarcely be distinguished, were it not for the differences in their wearing apparel.

Our knowledge of the existence of the planet Voris, once about 248 millions of miles from the sun, and of the fate which eventually overtook that body, we owe to the untiring efforts of those two intrepid scientists, Moody and Bedworth. There was widespread skepticism when, in 1971, they announced the completion of a rocket-propelled vessel in which they intended to undertake a journey through space. Later, when the start was actually made, and the shining torpedo-shaped vessel went roaring into the heavens under the motive power of rapidly-recurring explosions from the seven steel tubes clustered about its tail, the two scientists were given up as lost. And, indeed, it seemed that the world was correct in its gloomy predictions; for more than three years passed without any news from the two adventurers. In the rush of events they and their experiment were well-nigh forgotten.

Then, one night in July, 1974, there came the startling information from the International Voice-Vision news broadcasts that Moody and Bedworth had brought their space flier to a safe landing at a point not far from the city of Phoenix, Arizona. The incredulity of the listeners gave way to astonished belief as the first reports were confirmed by officials of that city; and the television screens of the news service soon flashed views of the great welcome being staged there for the explorers. The subsequent revelations made by the two men provided excited comment and speculation throughout the scientific world for many months.

The findings of the two scientists, fantastic as they seemed at first, were indisputable; and to astronomers they brought definite proof of several previously-disputed theories, and a vast amount of valuable knowledge of the heavens, made possible by extensive photographic records of observations made on and near the surface of Mars. There were likewise many stereoscopic motion pictures, which gave detailed information of conditions on that body. We learned that it had once been populated by a race of beings whose intelligence and scientific achievement far surpassed our own.

Of prime interest to scientists was the proof of the origin of the planetoids or asteroids, long a matter of dispute. For a time there was considerable argument pro and con, certain astronomers refusing for many months to credit the evidence brought back by Moody and Bedworth. This was because this evidence reestablished a long-discarded theory of the early nineteenth century, which had been framed when the discovery of the planetoids Pallas and Juno led astronomers to the belief that these bodies were but fragments of an original large planet which had in some manner disintegrated.

This theory having later been abandoned, the scientists were loath to revise their opinions and revert to the earlier suppositions. But, eventually, the translations of Martian records of the distant past proved the case so strongly that it was necessary for the dissenters to join the growing ranks of those who accepted the conclusions of Moody and Bedworth.

Being modest and reticent men, the two scientists gave little expression to the hardships and dangers of their remarkable undertaking; so there is much that is still unknown regarding the adventures which must have been their lot during the three years they remained on the red planet. But much can be inferred from their writings; since these point to the necessity of much toil and the visiting of many widely-separated regions of Mars. Their reports regarding the temperature and climate likewise give an indication of the difficulties which must have been encountered during their stay. How they existed for so long on a body of such desolation can but be conjectured; though it is apparent from passages in several of their books that they lived mostly on the flesh of flying creatures—the only form of life on a world almost devoid of water. It is also presumed that their camp was near one of the polar caps where snow and ice was more or less abundant, and that their journeys to other regions were made in the tiny collapsible airplane they had carried in the space-ship when they left the earth. But, though the labors of Moody and Bedworth have produced weighty volumes which are valuable to the scientific world, the language is technical and the conclusions coldly analytical, leaving the romantically inclined reader untouched, if indeed he can be persuaded to read a single volume to its conclusion.

How they located the ruins of many Martian cities and excavated for relics and records of the prosperous past ages seemed to the explorers to be of little consequence to the world; for they laid stress only on the final results of their labors. What captures the popular imagination is the unearthing, on the site of La-dar, which was learned to have been the greatest of all Martian cities, of a huge case in which the most amazing series of records imaginable had been preserved for the edification of future generations. This case was constructed of non-corrosive metal and had been hermetically sealed; so that the contents had been retained perfectly in their original condition for more than five thousand centuries of earth time. These records comprised the most valuable discoveries of the scientists, and have inspired most of their writings.

To the lay mind it seems incredible that, at a time when no higher form of life than the ape-men of Java existed on earth, the discoveries of the Martians were far in advance of our highest present-day accomplishments. But the records themselves prove this to be the case beyond shadow of doubt; and the clever manner in which they were prepared for the use of any intelligent beings who found them is a thing at which to marvel. When Moody and Bedworth first opened the metal case they were nonplussed by the many complicated mechanisms it contained; and we know that more than a year was required merely to learn the uses of the various portions of the apparatus. There were hundreds of reels of fine wire of extreme toughness and brilliant polish, and it was discovered only after much painstaking labor that these reels were intended for use in bringing the machine to life as a medium of carrying the thoughts of the ancient Martians to any future race that might be interested in them. Those who have witnessed the operation of this thought apparatus will never cease to marvel at the experience; for it is one that defies duplication by any agency that we possess.

Each reel of wire is a book, and when it is run through the Martian machine its story is clearly conveyed to the mind of the observer in pictures and in speech. The process is telepathic and, when the proper connections are made to helmets worn by the witnesses, it seems as if they are actually living in the times portrayed. With eyes closed, the observer is cognizant of living pictures presented as clearly as on the television screen, and spoken words are conveyed to his brain as in his own language.

THE author was particularly fortunate in winning the confidence of Harley Bedworth and in examining many of the "books" of the ancient Martians. These experiences have been of the highest interest, and have given rise to a determination to bring to the world the story possessing the greatest romantic interest. This tale has been robbed of much of its human appeal in the telling by the matter-of-fact Moody and Bedworth.

Perhaps the messages of these ancient reels of wire are conveyed in different manners to different minds; which may account for the overemphasizing of technical details and the lack of romance in the works of Moody and Bedworth, as well as for the reversal of this order of things by the author. However, if the reader so desires, he may compare the present work with that of the scientists* and may thus assure himself of the accuracy of the descriptions and the historical events recorded in this story.

It is hoped that the narrative will prove interesting and instructive to those who have neither the time nor the patience to make a technical study of the vastly superior writings of the two men who actually explored the planet once known to its inhabitants as Arin.

---

* "Origin of Worlds" – Moody and Bedworth (Yale Univ. Press, 1976)

Allow me to say in conclusion that one of the greatest difficulties experienced by the explorers in interpreting the Martian history was in unraveling the numbers and quantities referred to. From all the studies and evidence accumulated the Martian system of time was reckoned on their own year of 684 days. Their days were grouped in units or weeks of 12, there being 57 weeks. Each day was divided into 12 parts. Their day was approximately of the same duration as our own. Their numerical system also was based on units of twelve. So for convenience we will in this story call 12 of anything a unit.

CHAPTER ONE
The Prince of Marida

TORVEG XI, mighty monarch of all Marida, gazed thoughtfully from a window of his chambers in the great palace of La-dar. He was alone; and his meditations were on the glory of the past and of the possibilities in the future for his beloved country, the most powerful and prosperous in all Arin. There came to him a sense of gratification as he watched the rapid comings and goings of those of his people who rode the moving ways far beneath him. Raising his eyes to the heavens, he was further pleased by the sight of an unusual number of graceful aircraft which sped about in endless procession. His reign had been for Marida the happiest and richest since the great war with Voris during the rule of his ancestor, Torveg VII. And, with the completion of the latest extension of the main canals which provided his peoples with an increased supply of water, the future seemed indeed bright. When the time came, he thought, he would relinquish the throne of his forefathers with the comforting assurance that he had kept his trust well.

The occasion for this meditation was a momentous one; for on this day his only son Ronal, heir to the throne, reached his manhood. And Torveg was at this moment awaiting the appearance of the handsome and active youth whose early life had given such great promise. A worthy son was Ronal—a man after his father's own heart.

In his own chambers the young prince was submitting to the final ministrations of a man-servant who took every effort on this important morning to see that his young master was looking his very best. For Barlo had attended the young man since nursery days and was inordinately fond of him. He had, besides, a measure of professional pride in the appearance of his master; and, when he had finished his work, Barlo stepped back to view the results.

"Your Highness is positively magnificent," he breathed ecstatically. "When the ladies of the court set eyes upon you, they will lose their hearts *en masse.*"

Ronal laughed delightedly. "Barlo, you old sinner," he retorted, "it must be that you have a very great favor to ask. For you were ever a flatterer when about to request a day off."

"Oh no, Your Highness," objected the valet, with an injured air. "You have but to survey yourself in the glass to observe that I speak truth."

And indeed, the young prince presented an appearance in his new habiliments that would delight the eyes of all. Fully twice as tall as a table (over six feet) his body was as straight and sinewy as that of any athlete in the dominion the close-fitting uniform of deep red served to show to greatest advantage the perfection of his physique. The strength of his lean bronzed features was accentuated by the exceedingly highbrow and close-cropped thatch of chestnut hair which surmounted a perfectly-shaped head. The corners of his mouth drew upward in an amused quirk as he observed the worshipful expression in the eyes of Barlo.

"Are you sure you have no special favor to ask?" he inquired with a grin.

"Well, Your Highness," returned Barlo sheepishly, "now that you mention it, I should like your assurance that my services will be continued throughout your travels."

"Why, you old fox! I knew you wanted something. But, if that is the extent of your desire, you may rest easy. I could not do without you."

With that remark Ronal turned on his heel and went to meet his father, leaving Barlo in an ecstasy of pleasure over the pronouncement.

Torveg was aroused from his reverie by the click of heels close by, and he turned from the window to observe his son, standing at attention with his closed right fist pressed to his forehead in the royal salute.

"Salute me not, my son," said Torveg, "for from this day forth you are your own master. Today you assume your rightful place in the house of Torveg, and in the future you will receive the royal salute from our people, even as do I."

"It shall be as you say," responded Ronal, snapping his right hand smartly to his side and advancing to his father's chair, "but I fear that I still have much to learn regarding the responsibilities and prerogatives of my position. I trust you will bear with me during my novitiate."

"My son, I shall be pleased to tolerate much from you, should the necessity arise. But I am certain that there will be no such necessity. I am proud of you, my boy, and have great hopes for you. You have been a comfort and a joy to me since your dear mother left us; and I know that you will prove an even greater source of comfort and strength in my declining years. I shall miss you greatly while you are away."

"Must I leave at once?"

"It is the law, Ronal. For two years you must travel throughout the dominion, living in close contact with our people and sharing their joys and their sorrows, that you may be better prepared for the leadership that is to be yours. It is likewise decreed, as a preliminary, that you visit Voris incognito and learn what you can of the peoples of Keron."

Ronal's eyes shone eagerly. He had long looked forward with keen anticipation to that visit to distant Voris. "I understand fully, father," he replied. "And I shall endeavor to uphold the honor of our house in every sense. I, too, will miss the companionship which has been ours—your affection and counsel as well. But the separation is only in the flesh and is not for long. By means of the thought-projectors we can remain in daily contact."

"Yes, that is true." Torveg's voice brightened at the thought! "And now, my son, run along to the garden—Andites awaits you."

So Ronal, after a word of cheer, left Torveg to his meditations and hastened to the garden for the appointment with his tutor.

IN his accustomed seat beneath the bower of purple *ydrac* sat Andites, and he greeted Ronal with unusual warmth when that exuberant youth came upon him.

"Ronal, dear lad," he said; somewhat sadly, when their greetings were over, "your education is completed."

The gray-haired philosopher and scientist who had tutored the young prince since his early childhood gazed long and earnestly into the clear gray eyes of his pupil. What he saw there was good, and he drew a contented sigh as he awaited the reply of the suddenly solemn youth.

"BUT, Andites," came Ronal's objection, "there is still very much to be learned. Surely we are not to be separated now."

"You have uttered words of wisdom beyond your years. Truly there is much to be learned. A lifetime is entirely too short a period in which to absorb all knowledge. But, from this time forth, your knowledge must be obtained by actual contact with life, with the activities and the customs of Arin. My instruction is finished. It is but the foundation of that greater knowledge that will accrue to you during the years to come. You and I are to separate, insofar as our intimate association of the past is concerned. But think you not that

Andites is passing from your life. It is true that I shall no longer reside in the palace, but you must never forget that in my own humble home I shall be available at all times. In any crisis that may appear in your life, Andites is to be relied upon for advice and guidance. Come to me often, lad."

"Indeed I will." The boy's voice was serious. He felt a genuine affection for Andites, and was much perturbed over the realization that he was no longer to have him as a daily companion and mentor. "And will I not be able to keep in touch with you by means of the thought-projector?" he inquired anxiously.

"Most assuredly; I will look forward to frequent calls from you, wherever you may be. But, before we take our farewells, there is one point regarding which I wish to caution you. This is a matter of grave import and I have never spoken of it before in your presence. When I have finished I wish you would lock my words in your memory for future reference, so that you may be guided in forming your own opinions and in preparing for the inevitable in the years to come."

Ronal gave close attention, for never had Andites spoken to him in this manner. "Of what is it that you wish to speak?" he inquired.

"Of the future of Arin and of Voris. Even though I shall touch upon the probability of another war between the planets, there is a still more serious problem concerning which I shall not advise you until a full year has passed. There are many who think of Andites as an alarmist and who do not agree with his predictions of another interplanetarian war in the near future. But such a war will certainly come; and when you are traveling on the planet Voris you must make every effort to determine for yourself the approximate time of the intended invasion of our world and the means to be used in attacking us."

"Is this fact?" asked the astonished youth. "Why, it seems well-nigh incredible. My father, I am sure, anticipates no such thing. And what possible reason should the Vorisians have for attacking Arin? We are a peaceable people."

"It *is* fact. But you must keep your own counsel until you are able to see for yourself. Full well do I know that your most respected sire does not see matters in this light; but I tell you, lad, that this war is coming, as surely as you were born. The reason is jealousy; and the war lords of Keron are but awaiting an excuse to descend upon us in force as they did in the days of old."

"Well—this is most astonishing," stammered Ronal. "Of what can the Vorisians be jealous?"

"Of our remarkable progress during the past four generations. Remember, my lad, that our civilization is but twelve thousand years old while that of the people of Voris has developed through nearly twenty thousand years. A hundred years or more ago we were far behind them in learning and in accomplishment; but since the Great War the position has been reversed. Arin has developed intellectually by leaps and bounds, while Voris has retrogressed. Theirs is becoming a debased and decadent civilization, though they have every advantage in natural resources. This is enough for now, dear Ronal. Keep these thoughts in mind when you are among the peoples of Voris. Examine well the possibilities there. Farewell, my boy."

"Farewell, my Andites." And the younger man's eyes grew misty as he touched his forehead to that of his tutor in the manner of the people of Arin. He turned quickly away and no further words were spoken by either; for it was not considered good form, among the Arinian upper classes, to display melancholy emotions.

Ronal returned to the palace a much-sobered youth, and the words of Andites sank deep in his consciousness.

CHAPTER TWO
Ronal's Departure

THERE followed several days of feasting and celebration of Ronal's birthday in the palace and throughout the city of La-dar. But Ronal had not the interest in the proceedings that he had anticipated. He was too impatient to start on his journey to Voris; and the flattering attentions of the feminine members of the court bored him to exasperation. Barlo had been right in his predictions and, as Ronal humored one after another of the fair charmers, he became more and more convinced that women were sentimental fools. But then, he was a great student, and he had never found much time for the other sex. So it was hardly to be expected that he should change his inclinations in so short a time. Then, too, the parting words of Andites had so impressed him that he could think seriously of little else.

At last came the night of his departure. Ronal was as excited as Barlo, who fussed with the preparations in ill-concealed nervousness. It had been arranged that the young prince should travel as an ordinary engineering student, gathering the data required for post-graduate degrees. Torveg's councilor had signed a passport stating this. Ronal was attired in the customary garb of the character he had assumed, and Barlo retained his usual role of valet.

"All is in readiness, Your Highness," panted Barlo as he closed the last baggage case.

"Here, this will never do," admonished Ronal. "You must remember I am no longer 'Your Highness'—just plain 'Mattis'. That is the name on our passport, and you must be very careful to make no slips, or we shall find ourselves in difficulties."

"Very well—er—Mattis. But it seems entirely too familiar. I find it very difficult to address you in this manner but, never fear, I shall not forget."

Ronal laughed. "You should not feel embarrassed at the seeming familiarity, Barlo, after tending me so carefully these many years. But come, we must depart."

So, after taking hasty but affectionate leave of Torveg, Ronal hurried to the uppermost surface of the palace, where one of the speedy wingless aircraft of Marida awaited him. Barlo had preceded him and their baggage was already stowed away. The start was made immediately and they were soon high above La-dar, speeding towards Mi-ran, whence they were to set forth on the journey through space.

The first leg of the trip was over none too quickly for the two adventurers. Beneath them was Mi-ran. The little ship they occupied dropped rapidly to a landing among many others of, its kind in the extensive field beside the great humming power plant of the interplanetarian transportation system.

"I do not quite understand this new method of traversing space," said Barlo, gazing aloft at the huge steel building which housed the whirring machinery. "As I have heard, there are none of the old ships used now in making the voyage."

"You understand correctly," replied Ronal as they stepped from the cabin of their small craft and proceeded to the entrance of the vast structure. "The older method of traveling in torpedo-shaped vessels with rocket propulsion was entirely too slow for our modern requirements. We now make the trip to Voris by means of a beam or ray of complicated vibrations that travel to our destination at one hundredth the speed of light. (1,860 miles per second)

"Our ships are actually hurled through space at such a terrific rate?" asked Barlo apprehensively.

"Yes. But you will not be conscious of it, nor is there any danger in the process. You see, these complicated vibrations actually establish a magnetic beam composed of a stream of electrons across space. On this powerful beam the ship travels."

"But suppose something should happen to the beam? Suppose, for instance, the beam should miss its mark?" Barlo was not exactly comfortable in mind.

Ronal shrugged his broad shoulders. "Nothing ever happens. The beam cannot miss its mark, for there are powerful attracting forces at work on the other end which correct any errors in direction and assure the impingement of the ray of vibrations on the collector of the receiving apparatus. You need have no fear."

They had entered the large outer office and, after the passport had been scrutinized and approved, they were taken in charge by a guard and conveyed rapidly to the top level of the great building. By this time their ears had become accustomed to the roar of the machinery, and they were surprised to find that it now came to them as a not unmusical hum with a throbbing undertone that seemed somehow to steady the nerves.

They emerged on a balcony which overlooked the huge engine room, where not less than twelve great generators were in operation. These generators, the guard explained in reply to Ronal's interested inquiry, were delivering the quantity of operating power required. Truly, vast amounts of energy were needed in the remarkable process used in providing rapid transit facilities between Arin and Voris. The many generators were driven by individual motors of a type familiar to Ronal, compact atomic engines using as their fuel small quantities of ordinary rock, the disrupting atoms of which provided the tremendous driving energy with but little expenditure of the cheap and plentiful material.

After a thorough physical examination by a number of specialists, they were passed to the transmitting platform,"?" which was an immense circular flooring that occupied the greater portion of the roof space on the building. The circular area was illuminated by flood lights and in the exact center there was an enormous bowl of glistening metal. This bowl was mounted on a turntable which incorporated double trunnion supports, and the open surface of the bowl tilted at an angle of about sixty degrees with the horizontal. At the side of the bowl was a large reflecting telescope with its latticed length of tube pointed in the direction faced by the open mouth of the polished bowl. On the bowl was a large spherical ship, its door already open and admitting the oncoming passengers.

"Here," said the guard, "you may see the planet to which you are traveling."

HE directed them to the eyepiece of the telescope, and Ronal thrilled at the view of the surface of Voris as it appeared in its brilliant splendor. The magnification was so great that the field of vision included only a small portion of the face presented toward Arin. He could distinguish clearly a rugged sea-coast and a series of mountain ranges, through which two broad rivers wound toward the ocean. Covered by the crossed hairs in the exact center was an irregular splotch which the guide told him was Kir, capital city of Keron. Barlo followed his master in viewing the image and he was giving vent to exclamations of amazement, when their ears were assailed by a terrifying sound which emanated from the bowl beside them! They turned startled eyes to the guide, who smiled and ran rapidly up the steps of a nearby platform, motioning for them to follow.

The passengers had all entered the sphere and it awaited only our two travelers before departing. Looking up, they could see an intense purple beam stretching through the night toward a faintly twinkling star that they knew was Voris.

Hastily entering the car they took the cushioned couches made ready for them.

The sound from the bowl rose in pitch until it reached a screaming note that well-nigh shattered the ear drums. Then it vanished as it reached supersonic frequencies and the ensuing silence came as a distinct shock. Brighter glowed the bowl until its rose colored radiations bathed the sphere from top to bottom. The polished inner surface of the bowl reflected the light with dazzling brilliance.

Then there was a thump, a wrench as of the warping of the universe, and they felt themselves free in space, "Comfortable?" came into Ronal's ears from the phone beside his couch.

"Quite," replied Ronal. He smiled at Barlo questioningly. But Barlo did not answer. He was terrified into speechlessness and lay panting on his cot.

"You are extremely fortunate," came the voice of the unseen attendant, "for Arin and Voris are approaching conjunction at the present time. The distance is but 120,000,000 miles and the journey now requires less than a day."

Ronal raised his head to gaze skyward and, when he made out the brilliant point of light that was Voris, he wondered what the succeeding half-year in that far-off world held for them. Somehow, he felt a foreboding of grave complications, but his heart beat faster in anticipation of the adventures to come.

Then came a sense of drowsiness. His head felt very heavy and he sank into a sweet dreamless sleep.

CHAPTER THREE
Voris

"A DAY—a hundred years!" Ronal found himself repeating the words over and over, under his breath. Then suddenly he realized that he was awake and that something obstructed his vision. He remembered rising from his couch, he saw Barlo standing by him. Their luggage was being carried outside by a guard. Following with a feeling of great physical vigor that follows a refreshing sleep, Ronal found himself in brilliant sunshine instead of the glare of floodlights. They had arrived at the landing tower of Kir.

Surrounding them was a metallic ring a hundred feet or more in diameter, from which was suspended a sort of a net of woven cords. In the center of the net was a small platform and it was on this platform that the travelers had arrived. Shouts came to them from below in the language of Keron. Ronal peered through the mesh of the net and saw that they were but a short distance above a large field where a number of the inhabitants were busy at the controls of a derrick-like machine.

"We are here, Barlo," he said, shaking the dazed man into wakefulness.

Still unbelieving, his companion looked dazedly about him. Then he brightened perceptibly. "Why, so we are," he said in a relieved voice. "I thought we were in the land of lost souls, but it seems I was wrong." He bustled about in a sudden accession of energy, loading their baggage into a cage which now dangled at the side of the platform.

They were soon swung out over the edge of the ring and lowered to the ground, where a surly official surveyed them suspiciously and made careful examination of the passport. But everything was in order, and they were passed through a gate into an open space where a number of public aerocabs were in waiting for arriving passengers. Of course, Ronal had learned thoroughly the language of Keron and was thus able to make his wants known without difficulty. He selected a cab and ordered the pilot to convey them to the best hotel in Kir.

The air vehicle of Keron was but slightly different from those of Marida; obtaining its lifting force by means of a similar gravity-neutralizing field and being propelled by the discharge of expanding gases from a point beneath the tail. They rose quickly to a moderate altitude and headed for the city of Kir, the walls and towers of which could be discerned in the distance. The visitors experienced a slight sense of discomfort; for it was considerably warmer here than in their own land and the humidity was far higher. But otherwise they observed little difference from conditions on Arin, though the sun was shining less brightly here by reason of their greater distance from the luminary.

"Do you desire to encircle the city before landing at the hotel?" inquired the pilot, who seemed to be friendly enough.

"Yes, that is a good suggestion," agreed Ronal. "It will give us an opportunity to orient ourselves."

"You have never visited Voris?"

"Never. And we are looking forward to it with much pleasure."

"Well, you have arrived at a good time. In the city of Kir the celebration of Matara is now being observed—one of our holidays, you know—and there is much merry-making. We shall pass over the amphitheater where Olar is now reviewing his mounted guard."

Ronal translated rapidly to Barlo, who displayed keen interest in the news. This entire trip was more or less of a holiday to the middle-aged man who had left the city of La-dar but three times during his entire lifetime. But the young prince was not so enthusiastic; for Andites had told him of some of the orgies of the Keronians when on holiday.

The air was filled with pleasure craft, and beneath them spread a city of a size fully as great as La-dar. Its upper moving ways were crowded with people in holiday attire. The high walls surrounding Kir were bedecked with emblems and banners of many colors, as were the myriad aircraft that darted and circled about them on every side. Now they shot past a tall spire, which rose from the upper surface of the city to so great a height that its pointed tip seemed to be but a few feet beneath them. The pilot advised Ronal that this was the spire which surmounted the palace of Olar, ruler of all Keron, and thus, by overlordship of the mightiest nation, the actual dictator of his entire world.

Now they were over the main thoroughfare of the city, a broad central lane of traffic on either side of which rose the larger buildings of Kir. These, unlike the pleasingly-decorated edifices of La-dar, were monotonously uniform in construction, and of neutral hued, non-corrosive metal. Were it not for the holiday decorations, thought Ronal, this city of Kir would indeed present a drab and uninteresting appearance to the eye of the cultured visitor from Arin. Ahead of them, the central roadway terminated in a large circular area which they soon made out as the amphitheater of which the pilot had spoken. Then they were directly overhead; and the cab dropped still lower and hovered about to permit them to witness the scenes beneath.

In the exact center of the arena was a large dais, upon which sat Olar and his royal party in the midst of his courtiers and ministers. The stands were packed with his subjects, and the gesticulations and flag-waving of the multitude viewed from above produced the effect of a restless body of water. In a circular track, which occupied the entire space between the dais and the stands, paraded the royal guard, several hundred brightly plumed soldiers mounted on *yaraks,* those swift-footed striped quadrupeds whose breed had been perpetuated through the ages. The maneuvers of the perfectly-trained troops proved of interest for some little time and then, suddenly very tired, Ronal directed their pilot to convey them to the hotel. The effect of the sleeping gas given to them on the journey was beginning to wear off.

The little aerocab carried them to their destination and dropped lightly to the flat roof of one of the larger structures on the main thoroughfare. Here they were welcomed by one of the uniformed employees of the huge hotel who took their luggage and guided them to an elevator which carried them to the floor where they had their rooms. After partaking of a satisfying repast, quite similar to one of their usual meals at home, they retired to the elegant suite to which they had been assigned and prepared to secure a more natural rest.

RONAL did not know that he had slept through the re-mainder of the day and the entire night, when he was awakened by an insistent musical note which emanated from an instrument reposing on the small table at his bedside. The door leading to Barlo's room was closed; else that perfect servant would long since have replied to the summons of the thought-projector which had roused his master.

Who could be calling him, in this land where he was en-tirely unknown? Who, excepting Barlo, knew his identity? Startled into complete wakefulness by these questions, Ronal sat up and touched the button which indicated his acceptance of the call. Then he stepped to the instrument and adjusted the cap that would carry the thought impulses from his unexpected communicant to his own consciousness. A small square of light appeared on the box of the apparatus, as the electrodes on the inner surface of the cap made contact with his temples. In this square of light appeared the face of a beautiful girl whose features betrayed anxious concern.

Quick as a flash came the thought waves that answered his own unspoken questions.

"It matters not who I am, or how I learned the stranger known as Mattis, is not what he seems," came the thoughts of the charming young woman. "Suffice it to say that I am also a native of La-dar and am in favor at the court of Olar. It has come to my ears that one Mattis was placed under suspicion at the receiving station of the space traversing ray, and that danger awaits him. You must leave Voris at once."

Indeed he would not leave Voris! He had just arrived and had a half year of adventure before him! He would—

"Think not too deeply," interrupted the thoughts of the other, "or you will betray your true identity. And even I, who am your compatriot, have no desire to know who you really are or why you are here. But go—go at once from this place. Leave Kir—leave Voris entirely!"

With a fleeting smile from the imaged face, the square of light went dark and a sharp click from the mechanism indicated that the radiant energy from the unknown transmitter no longer actuated the instrument. Ronal raged and fumed, but there was nothing he could do. Not knowing who his fair informant was or where she might be found, he had no means of calling back or of learning more details concerning the strange warning. But he was determined that his stay in Kir was not to be shortened by so vague an admonition.

"Barlo!" he called impatiently. "Barlo!"

"What is it, Your Highness?" replied the valet as he hastily thrust his head through the quickly-opened door.

"May the imps of the dry lands take you!" stormed Ronal. "Must I warn you anew that I am Mattis?"

"I am very sorry—Mattis," quavered Barlo, astonished at the unwonted display of ill humor on the part of his master. "I am still not fully awake and am therefore not alert to my responsibilities."

"It is my fault, Barlo," conceded the young prince, "but an anonymous call over the thought-projector has put me in a rather beastly humor. A warning to leave Voris—what think you of that?"

"A warning?" Barlo's eyes opened wide in fear for the safety of his young master. "Some man of Kir knows that you are the son of—but I shall not repeat it. They know who you are?"

"No, but someone knows that I am not Mattis. And it is a woman, not a man."

"A woman? A woman of Kir?"

"No. This one, young and beautiful, claims she is from La-dar and the warning she sent is friendly. But she gave no details other than that it is officially suspected that Mattis is not as he seems to be, nor as his passport implies."

Barlo trembled and his kindly face went white. "We shall leave immediately?" he anxiously inquired.

"Indeed not!" barked Ronal, removing his sleeping garments and entering the room of the cold mist shower. "We shall remain. It is permitted by the treaty that a freeman of Arin may visit Voris twice during his lifetime. I shall not be frightened away."

He snorted and puffed in the cold water-mist that enveloped him, his usual good humor quickly restored. But Barlo's spirits sank and a sense of gloomy foreboding came over him. Silently he laid out his master's wearing apparel for the day and silently he returned to his own room.

CHAPTER FOUR
The Summons from Olar

IMMEDIATELY following the morning meal, Ronal inquired in the office of the hotel regarding the purchase of a private aerocab and was given the necessary instructions. With Barlo at his heels, he left the hotel at the seventh level and entered upon the moving ways of the main thoroughfare. They stepped quickly from the slow-moving outer way, across two of gradually increasing speed until they reached the fourth, and fastest, which carried them rapidly toward the shop to which they had been directed. Above and below them many levels of similar ways rushed noiselessly in both directions, carrying the populace of Kir about their daily affairs. It was quite like a scene in the lower levels of La-dar; but here the people with whom they rubbed elbows were dressed so lightly; in fact, Ronal thought, almost immodestly. Their faces bore the marks of riotous living. The words of Andites recurred to the young prince with ever increasing import.

They soon reached the establishment where the speedy aircraft of Keron might be obtained through the medium of exchange agreed upon in the ancient treaty with Arin. The purchase was quickly made, and a sleek, four-passenger cabin-craft was conveyed to the landing stage on the roof of the building.

"Do you require the services of a pilot?" inquired the salesman.

"No," replied Ronal, in the language of Keron, "I am considered an expert pilot in my own land. But I shall require a chart of the surface of Arin."

"That we can provide. But have you a license'?"

"A license?" Here was an unexpected obstacle, "I was not aware that a license was necessary."

"It is a new law. We cannot deliver the machine unless you have one."

"Does the obtaining of such a license involve much difficulty?" asked Ronal.

"None. Being a visitor from Arin, it will merely be necessary for you to present your passport at the license bureau and give evidence of your ability to handle the type of craft purchased."

So it was arranged that a pilot be supplied to carry them to the Aircraft Registration Department where the required papers would be obtained. But Barlo was nervously apprehensive of any procedure which involved further examination of their passport by officials of the government, and he did not hesitate to communicate his fears to Ronal while their vessel was being made ready for the start.

"Yes, that has occurred to me too," whispered Ronal, "but we must go through with it now and trust to good fortune that nothing develops. Probably all will be well."

But all was not well, for when they reached the proper officials and Ronal presented his passport, together with an application for a license, there was a considerable delay. Barlo's nervousness increased as time wore on and the official did not return with the credentials. But Ronal was already thinking of rushing to the landing stage on the roof and overpowering the hired pilot, if necessary, when the official returned with the passport and a metal tag.

"This," he announced, "is a temporary permit. There is some confusion regarding your passport and we had instructions this morning from the prime minister that a first class license was not to be issued to Mattis of La-dar. There was the further message that you are to report to the prime minister in the palace of Olar at your earliest opportunity. However, the permit will allow you to navigate your own craft over the city of Kir without molestation, so you will be able to go to the palace. It is my advice that you do this immediately; as the premier will be able to straighten out your papers in short order and you will then be able to proceed where you will."

Ronal's wrath rose apace at the official's suave words; but he wisely refrained from showing it. Accepting the permit and the return of his passport, he proceeded to the landing stage and dismissed the pilot who had brought them. He seated himself at the controls of the new craft and, when Barlo had closed the door, jerked the vessel skyward with a savage wrench of the gravitation lever.

"By the brain* of my ancestors," he swore, "this outrage shall be avenged! It is incredible that a son of the house of Torveg should be refused the normal courtesies of this outlandish country. I must report to the premier! Indeed!"

"Was that the request of the official'?" asked Barlo.

"Yes. In fact, it was practically an order. He said there is some irregularity in the passport and I am granted only a temporary permit." Ronal was raging, and they shot swiftly aloft through a bank of heavy clouds which hid the city from their view.

"Do you not intend to report—Mattis?" asked Barlo, glancing in all directions for signs of danger.

"I do not. We are going away from here—now. Hand me that chart of Voris."

---

*This is not quite exact. Ronal probably refers to the telepathic organ of their race, located in the base of the skull.

But this rash resolve was never carried out, for, at that moment, there came the screech of a siren close by and a government vessel drew alongside. The etherphone of the new craft spoke loudly at Ronal's ear.

"Are you Mattis of La-dar?" came the inquiry from the larger ship.

"I am," replied Ronal in a surly voice.

"We have orders to bring you to the palace at once— orders from Olar himself. You are to be interviewed by his prime minister."

"Am I under arrest?"

"Not unless you make such a regrettable action necessary. And we do not believe you will do that. Few have dared to disobey when Olar commands."

Ronal peered through the transparent cabin walls at the speaker and saw that he was armed. He likewise observed that there were no less than eight other officers in the large ship, and that grim determination was written on the features of each.

He decided that he must capitulate.

"Very well," he grunted in the gutturals of the Keronian tongue. "Lead on, and I shall follow."

"THINGS begin to look discouraging, Barlo." Ronal commented, as the police ship of Keron dived into the clouds and he dropped his own vessel in its wake. "I cannot understand the meaning of all this nor why it is that I should be under suspicion at all."

"What can they do?" asked Barlo.

"Legally—nothing. Of course there is the provision of the treaty that no members of the royal families of either planet may visit the other, but no penalties are attached. Besides, there is the precedent established when Nur, father of this Olar, visited Arin incognito and was discovered. Our people overlooked that incident; but there is no reason why my visit should raise such a tremendous furor in Kir if I am discovered. But still—I wonder."

"How could they have possibly known of your coming'?"

"That is likewise a mystery. Still, they have evidently kept very close watch over us since our arrival, and it may be that there are spies in our own land. Perish the thought! And yet—!"

"You suspect something'?" asked Barlo, realizing his, master's indecision.

"I am beginning to. And I may as well tell you, Barlo, that Andites warned me of impending trouble between the two planets. It appears that he was correct in his assumptions."

"Andites told you of this'? And still you came?"

"Most certainly. Think you that Ronal, son of Torveg, can be frightened by mere talk of wars and vague warnings of danger'? But we have arrived, Barlo. We shall soon see what is in store for us."

They circled the spire of the palace, dropped to a landing beside the police ship, and stepped from their vessel. Without delay they were conducted to the elevator and soon emerged at the end of a long corridor. From the far end of the magnificently-carpeted hall there came the sounds of music and of revelry; but their guards stopped at a great bronze door only a few steps from the shaft of the lift. In another moment they had stepped into the presence of the Mara.

Underneath a high arch, that separated the room they had entered from a second larger chamber, sat the sinister Catin Mara of Keron and trusted adviser of Olar. He glanced at Ronal and Barlo with bleared and shifty eyes that peered from beneath bristling brows in a furtive manner that was far from comforting. With a curt nod he dismissed the guards.

"You sent for Mattis of La-dar?" asked Ronal haughtily.

"I sent for him who carries the passport of Mattis," returned Catin with an unpleasant grimace. "Do you claim to be a student from Arin?"

"I do. And, if you will be so good as to examine my credentials, you will find them in order." With a disdainful gesture Ronal cast the scroll on the desk top.

As Catin examined the disputed document, Barlo fidgeted apprehensively, but Ronal gazed calmly beyond the bent head of the Mara into the larger chamber he had perceived. Then he received a shock; for between the heavy drapes at the far side of the inner room there appeared a vision of feminine loveliness such as he had never before encountered. Slender of body and fair of skin was the beautiful girl who faced him, and the dazzling smile she bestowed was a thing to remember forever. Her jet-black locks were encircled by a gold band and, just over the alabaster forehead, shone the jeweled emblem of the royal family of Keron. Silently she raised her arm and, with a graceful gesture, placed the tip of a finger to her lips. Then she stepped from the curtains and advanced to the side of Catin's desk.

Ronal's heart pounded unaccountably and Barlo peered quizzically at his master when he observed the sudden flush that mantled his features.

Catin, startled from his reading, looked up at the approach of the girl. And, when he had observed who she was, he jumped hastily to his feet.

"Your Highness!" he gasped, "I failed to hear you come in. Can I be of service to my Princess?"

"THE Princess!" thought Ronal. "No wonder they call her Ila the beautiful!"

Then an amazing thing occurred. The Princess Ila drew her hand from the folds of her garment and they saw that it held a gleaming object, at sight of which Catin paled and cried out in fright. But, before he could raise the alarm, a beam of purplish light darted from the weapon to his breast and he slumped to the floor.

"You have killed him!" said Ronal in astonishment.

"No, but he will sleep for many days. An unkinder fate was reserved for you. We must hurry!"

She opened the massive door and peered cautiously into the corridor, then beckoned them to follow. Ronal stepped to her side and Barlo advanced timidly at her heels, his worst fears confirmed. The long hall was empty, but from the shadows at its end came the sounds of wild and discordant music. The revelers were uproarious.

"It is well," approved Ila, as she listened to the noise.

"We will not be followed."

Then there came a terrified feminine scream from the shadows and the music was abruptly stilled. Ila grasped the arm of Ronal for support, uttering a single word in a panic-stricken voice:

"Mother!"

Sobbing with fright, she loosed her hold of Ronal's sleeve and raced madly along the corridor in the direction from which the scream had come. The two visitors from Arin, forgetting their own danger, followed closely behind.

CHAPTER FIVE
Olar's Crime

THE scene in the huge chamber at the end of the hall was one not easily forgotten. Fully two hundred scantily-attired Keronians were scattered about in various stages of the wild intoxication produced by the drug *cesal*.* On a raised platform in a corner of the great room was the throne of Olar and before it stood that mighty monarch, swaying drunkenly to and fro as he attempted to raise a feminine figure that lay before him. Ila ran across the room, stumbling over many a prostrate form as she made her way to the throne. With a violent thrust she toppled her almost helpless father into his heavily-cushioned seat. Then she knelt at the side of the prostrate woman and gently turned the face upward. She laid her cheek against that of her mother for a moment, and then sprang erect, her eyes flashing fire.

"Dead!" she shouted, advancing to the huddled figure of Olar. "You have murdered my mother, you beast! You and your vile court with your drunken revels! You are no father of mine, Olar the Great, and Ila warns you here and now to beware of your crown!"

With the palm of her tiny hand she struck the bloated face of the monarch. Then she knelt once more beside the still figure and burst into uncontrolled weeping. Unsteadily Olar rose to his feet, and as he did so a murmur of incredulity swept through the assemblage, for in his hand he still held the weapon with which he had brutally taken the life of his

---

*A Keronian plant that acted upon the brain in a similar fashion to alcohol.

consort. The murmur swelled to a roar as he advanced on Ila, and Ronal shouted aloud as he sprang from the shadows where he and Barlo had remained. But quick as he was, there were others ahead of him, and before he reached the side of Ila, a dozen of the younger nobles had rushed to her defense, Olar was down and was being held in a subjection such as he had never experienced in all his tyrannical career. Those brave nobles of Keron, for all their recent debauchery, drew a shout of admiration from Ronal, for well he knew that their lives were forfeit, and that they had willingly faced death to protect their beloved princess from the drunken violence of her royal father.

In the ensuing confusion Ronal and Barlo were unnoticed, and it was not long before Ila, pale and exhausted, extricated herself from the milling combatants and joined them.

"We must leave at once!" she panted. "The guards are even now on the way and wholesale slaughter will follow their appearance on the scene. Ila's life is now in as much danger as your own. Come!"

Even as she spoke there came a detachment of the guard and every exit was jammed with frantic Keronians attempting to escape. Ila pressed a slab in a panel of the nearby wall and a black opening gaped before them. She thrust the two men inside and almost fell over them as she followed and hastily closed the panel behind them, just as the hubbub in the room they had quitted reached the proportions of a panic.

"Mother, mother, poor mother!" she sobbed. "At last you have found peace."

Then the girl calmed herself and once more took charge of Ronal and Barlo. She led them step by step through the dark passage until they reached a winding stair. Up this they climbed endlessly, still in impenetrable darkness. None of them spoke until eventually, with a hiss of warning, Ila stopped and they could hear her fumbling with the fastenings of a door overhead. A slit of daylight appeared, and this widened to a considerable opening as Ila raised the trapdoor sufficiently for them to obtain a view of the outside.

"It is all right," she whispered. "Come!"

They followed her through the opening, and found themselves on the palace roof, close by the landing stage where stood Ronal's vessel. The stage was empty of Keronians; but the police ship still rested in the position in which it had landed. They hastened to the little cabin aerocar at Ila's direction and, when Ronal had opened the door, were surprised to see that another beautiful young woman had preceded them—the girl of the thought-projector warning!

"Mirsa, Mirsa!" exclaimed the princess, throwing herself into the arms of the other girl. "I am so glad you escaped! Did you see?"

"I saw, my poor Ila, and left immediately by the central lift. I foresaw the consequences and hurried to the rendezvous. But we must be off, before the news is broadcast."

"Yes, yes," agreed Ila, "at once." She turned to Ronal, "And you, Prince Ronal, must remove the weapons from the police ship. We shall need them."

Aghast at the knowledge that he was known, Ronal nevertheless hastened to obtain the weapons in the police car. With Barlo's assistance he quickly stripped the vessel of its armament, which included the hand-weapons that projected the deadly disintegrating ray and two heavier projectors that were capable of destroying a vessel of like size. These were conveyed to his own craft and, when they were all seated within and prepared for the start, it was found that the quarters were crowded to the limit. Ronal, with his fingers on the controls, looked inquiringly at Ila.

"Rise immediately to the highest safe altitude," she directed, "and then I will instruct you further."

She had procured the chart and was examining it carefully. The little craft responded quickly to Ronal's touch and soon rose high above the clouds which still covered the sky.

MANY things were explained during the rapid flight from Kir. Ila, though deeply grieved, succeeded in hiding her feelings, and she lost no time in making clear to the visitors from Arin the exact state of affairs. She had mapped out their course for Ronal, and the little vessel was now carrying them over the black ocean which separated Keron from Alata, whither they were bound.

"It is a long story, my Prince," she responded to Ronal's inquiries, "but I shall endeavor to make all things known to you. First, I must reiterate my statement that Olar is no father to me. I have long since renounced him for the misery and suffering he has brought to my dear mother during the past years. Now she is gone—the victim of his brutality— and I have another score to settle with him. Few there are in Keron, in fact in all Voris, few who are fit to live; and I hope and pray that in the coming war with Arin the entire breed is destroyed."

"A war is coming?" asked Ronal.

"It has been planned for many years. Spies are everywhere in the land of Marida and throughout all Arin. It was through the agency of these spies that Olar learned of your coming to Voris; and it was through Mirsa's influence with Olar that we discovered the fact that you had arrived. When Mirsa ended her thought-projector contact with you so abruptly this morning, she did so in fear that her thoughts would betray the certain knowledge of your identity and that you would then not report to the palace when ordered to do so.

"Keron has been retrogressing morally for many, many years and things have now become so bad that no woman— not even the daughter of Olar—is safe. And it is a sad commentary on the decadence of our race when I admit freely that few of the women are better than the men. When Mirsa came from Arin I found a friend I could trust, and she has been my constant companion since. Olar became enamored of her, and life has been more difficult since then. But his infatuation enabled her to learn many of the plans for war against Arin and also of your coming. We had planned for her to escape these intolerable conditions and return to Arin with you. But now it has become necessary for even Ila to leave her native world."

"FOR which I am very thankful," quoth Ronal, forgetting for a moment the sad cause of her exile. Ila looked deep into the eyes of this prince from distant Arin, and what she saw caused her to blush. She continued hastily:

"Arrangements had been completed for the stealing of one of the space ships from the great shipyards of Alata, and this ship is now awaiting our arrival. Its crew consists of but three Keronians in whom I have absolute confidence. One is Lyris, my personal maid since childhood. The other two are her husband and son, both Keronians of the strictest integrity—a rare virtue here, even among the servant classes. We shall be absolutely secure in their company, once we have escaped the atmosphere of Voris."

"You think we shall be attacked before we leave?"

"I hope not. But the alarm must have gone out by now, and I fear that Olar may suspect our destination and endeavor to head us off. In that case we must fight."

The coast line of Alata now came in view and Ronal changed his course slightly as they swung inland to follow the direction plotted by Ila. Beneath them they made out the heavy foliage of the wildernesses. Here and there, a city thrust its towers skyward through the thickness of the jungle. But they kept to an altitude far above the regular traffic lanes, and sped onward to the single hope of escape from the vengeance of Olar.

Soon they were in sight of the great shipyard where lay some twenty of the spherical space vessels which Ila had said were being groomed for the war against Arin. The etherphone was tuned to the frequency agreed upon with Ila's allies. A call was made and repeated, but no reply was received; and just then Barlo shouted out from his seat in the rear of the little vessel.

"A police ship!" he called. "Just above us, Your Highness!"

Ronal dropped the ship in a nose dive and came up rapidly, intending to rise above the larger and more unwieldy ship which had followed them. As he did so one of the disintegrating rays from the police ship grazed the nose of the vessel and opened in it a great jagged gap. Ila frantically repeated her calls over the etherphone as the tiny car climbed swiftly to meet the enemy. Mirsa helped Barlo to set up one of the larger ray projectors, and they soon succeeded in training it on the under surface of the police ship. There was a puff of bluish smoke from overhead and their pursuers were no more. But still there was no response from the etherphone, and as they now descended the shapes of two more police vessels appeared rapidly nearing them.

They were directly over the shipyard and could plainly see the shapes of the great spheres that clustered within its confines. A voice rang through their cabin.

"We are coming, Your Highness!" came the reassuring words, "We will pick you up aloft. Have your pilot land on our upper surface."

Then one of the shining globes left its fellows and came up quickly beneath them. But the two police ships were now searching the air around the tiny car with their deadly rays and Ronal resorted to every maneuver with which he was familiar to keep them from finding their mark. Barlo did his best to direct the ray from his own weapon but the darting of the smaller craft made it quite impossible to reach one of the police ships. Another contact with the hull of their own vessel, and its tail disappeared in a puff of bluish smoke. But the space flier was just beneath and, as Ronal dropped in a rather heavy landing, Ila called out in triumph. Her friends on the upper platform of the huge sphere had just trained on their pursuers rays from two long-range projectors. Two smoke puffs were all that remained of the police! The fugitives were hustled inside the spherical vessel, and the circular manhole was clamped shut behind them. A quick lurch told of the suddenly increased speed and they knew that the sphere was shooting skyward with tremendous velocity.

They were bound for Arin.

CHAPTER SIX
The Return of Ronal

WITH a five-day journey before them, the occupants of the space flier proceeded to make friends immediately. Barlo found much in common with Sulor, the husband of Lyris. Mirsa, even after the ice was broken, stood in great awe of Ronal and addressed him always as "Highness." But Ila conversed with him on terms of equality; and he soon discovered that she was a girl of unusual intelligence, and possessed of an education as extensive as his own. But for the first three days of the journey she confined herself to her rooms, with Lyris in constant attendance. Coming as a reaction after the excitement of the escape, the full realization of the passing of her mother struck her with overwhelming force and in her grief she chose to withdraw from the rest of the party. During this period Ronal spent a great deal of his time with Andon, son of Sulor, in the control room of the vessel, and he learned much regarding the recent activities of Olar.

Andon, it developed, had been employed in the shipyards of Alata for many years and was expert in the construction and operation of the spherical space fliers. These were modern developments of the older craft and resembled in many ways the ships used on the transportation beam. There were one hundred of the ships already built; and these had been distributed among five bases in isolated sections similar to the one in Alata.

When Lyris had advised him of the Princess Ila's determination to get Mirsa back to her own land, Andon obtained a position for his father in the shipyard and immediately laid plans for the appropriation of one of the spheres with which to make the trip. They knew that Olar would never permit Mirsa to leave by the transportation beam, since his passion for her was growing in intensity until it had reached the proportions of an obsession. Later, Lyris had joined her husband and son for a visit, and she was overjoyed when she learned that her beloved princess also was to leave Voris; though she deeply lamented the passing of Ania, the queen.

"But Andon," Ronal had objected, when they were still but a short distance from Voris, "how is it that none of the other space fliers have attempted to follow us? I should think that Olar would have the entire fleet out searching for us."

"The others are not prepared for flight—because one of the vessels was badly damaged a short time ago in a trip taken by some employees of the shipyard when they were under the influence of *cesal*. It was then decreed that all vessels be rendered useless by the removal of the exciters of the atomic motors!

"How then were you able to provide this ship with an exciter?"

Andon smiled, "The exciter is really quite simple; and father and I were able to construct one from odds and ends we found in the machine shop of this particular ship. We have kept this a secret, so nobody expected to see the *CXF* rise when it did. We left a rather surprised commander behind us."

"It would seem, however, that one or more of the other spheres could be quickly prepared for the chase," said Ronal.

"Nearly half a day would be required, and there would then be no chance of overtaking the *CXF*, for all of these ships have the same maximum speed. We have no fear of pursuit, Your Highness."

"The *CXF* is a duplicate of all other ships of the fleet?"

"It is. All have been built to the same specifications and drawings. The method of propulsion is the same as that used in the older vessels. Power is obtained by the atomic disintegration of ordinary shale in the motors. The gravity field is produced electrically and may be varied in intensity and direction, or reversed to utilize the gravitation of various bodies in the solar system when we require such changes to alter our course or speed. There are accommodations for two hundred fighting men aboard each vessel, in addition to the normal crew of six."

"Of what does the armament consist?"

"There are, of course, the hand weapons for the fighters, ordinary ray pistols capable of annihilating the human body at a distance of two hundred yards. Then there are two great beam generators on each ship, either of which could destroy the palace of Olar or of Torveg from a distance of more than a mile. In addition, there are various other beams, and some gas bombs with which I am not familiar. Some of these weapons are of comparatively recent development and their exact potentialities have been kept secret from the pilots and engineers. But, from small talk I have overheard, it is certain that they are of a terrifically destructive nature."

"It is evident that Olar intended to declare war in the very near future, Andon." Ronal paced the floor of the control room in deep thought.

"He has been waiting only for some excuse, such as your arrival in Voris. I have no doubt now that the fleet will visit Arin almost immediately—and without warning. Are your people prepared?"

"We are absolutely unprepared," replied Ronal solemnly. "We, of Arin have had no suspicion of the plotting of Olar. It was but a few days ago that I had the first hint of such a thing from my old tutor Andites, a noted physicist of La-dar. How he came to know of it is still a mystery to me."

"I greatly fear that Arin will prove an easy field for conquest, Your Highness."

"It would seem so, Andon." And Ronal became lost in meditation pondering the problem presented to the peace loving peoples of Arin.

EACH day these conversations in the control room brought new information to Ronal, and each day he grew more apprehensive of the result of Olar's plans and more impatient for the arrival in Arin. When they were still more than 60 million miles distant from his own world he attempted to get in touch with Andites by means of the thought-projector of the *CXF*, though he knew that they were entirely out of range of its low-power transmitter.

When, on the fourth day, Ila rejoined the party, it seemed that she had failed greatly in health; for she was hollow-eyed from loss of sleep, and her skin had taken on an alarming pallor. Lyris fussed about her continually, and Ronal's heart went out to the suffering of the unhappy girl.

"You have heard the worst?" she asked Ronal, as they conversed after their first meal together.

"I believe so. Andon has told me of the fleet and of what he knows of the plans of Olar. It seems that Arin is to become the scene of a terrible war."

"It will come very soon, I fear. But, from this time forth, Ila is no longer a Princess of Keron. Her sympathies are entirely with the people of Arin."

"BUT there will be great danger for you in La-dar."

Ila shrugged her pretty shoulders. "No more than in Kir, my Prince. In fact I shall quite probably be safer with your people than with my own."

Ronal thought of the scene in the palace of Olar and shuddered. "Yes, that is probably true," he agreed. "And Mirsa? What will become of her?"

"She has her people. Her father is a Bodin* in La-dar, and is in very comfortable circumstances. I am expecting to make my home with her, at least for a time."

"I had hoped you would consent to take up your abode in the palace of Torveg."

"No, dear Prince, that would never do. When the people of Arin learn of Olar's enmity they will hardly consent to the harboring of his daughter in the palace of Marida's ruler."

"But you are not an enemy," objected Ronal.

"I am a friend. And I hope to become more. I hope to become one of your people and to be happy among them— after the war is over."

"And I—I hope you will become even more than that." Again Ronal gazed deep into her eyes, and again Ila flushed, the spreading color covering the pallor from her beautiful features.

To hide his own embarrassment at the temerity of his words, Ronal stepped to the thought-projector and made another call for Andites. He was delighted at obtaining contact almost immediately, and lost no time in transferring all of his thoughts regarding the events of the past few days to the eagerly receptive mind of his old tutor.

"This confirms my own suspicions fully," came the unspoken thoughts of Andites, "and I shall take immediate action. I shall apprise Torveg at once and request him to call together the scientists of La-dar to devise means of defense. You arrive tomorrow?"

"Yes, and I shall proceed to the palace as soon as we land. You think we might be able to make a fair show of defense?"

---

*A local commissioner of the government.

"It is not very hopeful, at least for the first attack. But I am not sure they will be entirely successful. I have ideas, but those can wait. Immediate action is a must. Farewell, lad."

"Farewell, my Andites." And, somehow, Ronal was greatly encouraged by this contact. He turned to impart the news to Ila, but she had taken the opportunity to escape from the room.

Then followed the longest waiting Ronal had ever known. He found that he was unable to sleep, and, as a consequence, spent most of the rest period in the control room where Sulor was relieving Andon. Here, in the emptiness of space, there was neither day nor night. Or more accurately, one side of their spherical ship was always in daylight and the other side always in darkness. But regular sleeping and waking hours had been observed throughout the voyage, the time being based on a standard Vorisian chronometer. With its rays unobstructed by an atmosphere, the sun appeared as a vast ball of blinding magnificence, with brilliant streamers of flame extending in all directions far into space. Even at that enormous distance from the radiant center of the solar system, it was impossible to observe it with unprotected eyes. And, as soon as the eyes turned from the luminous body the blackness of the firmament seemed even more ebon by comparison; the stars and planets shining steadily and brightly like jewels set in a background of black velvet.

Then, when the others awakened, they gathered in the control room to join those who had spent so many hours within its confines. The orb of Arin was now large in the heavens, rushing madly to meet them. The north polar cap shone white in the glare of the sun and the great canals radiating from this point to irrigate the inhabited areas of the planet stood out blackly against the arid whiteness of the dry lands, monuments to the ingenuity and diligence of generations of Arinians.

Breakfast was forgotten in their absorption in the magnificent sight of the body as it drew so rapidly near them. The *CXF* seemed to hang motionless in space, as the great globe came so close that it filled their entire field of vision. Then, as they watched, there was no longer a globe but a vast bowl with the horizon as its rim. They had entered the atmospheric envelope of Arin and the speed of the ship was greatly reduced. Soon they were within a few thousand feet of the surface, over the dry lands at a point not many miles from Mi-ran, whence Ronal and Barlo had started their journey.

Ronal obtained thought-projector contact with Torveg and received enthusiastic and affectionate greeting. But in the rejoicing of his father there was an undertone of sadness and misgiving.

Soon they were very close to Mi-ran and Ronal pointed out to Ila the great power plant of the transportation beam, its bowl-shaped reflector gleaming in the sun and the ring of the receiving net clearly outlined against the green of the adjoining field. Even as they watched, there was an appalling concussion and the entire plant vanished in a cloud of smoke and hurtling particles that reached nearly to the *CXF;* which was rocked so violently by the blasts that they were compelled to hold to the control panels and ceiling supports to keep from being hurled to the floor. They stared aghast as the debris from the terrific explosion settled, and the smoke cleared away to reveal an enormous crater where the plant and the city had stood.

It was Olar's first blow. A car of powerful explosives transported over the beam had detonated on arrival, forever cutting off this means of communication, and causing great damage and loss of life. In awed silence the little party remained, while the *CXF* sped toward La-dar.

CHAPTER SEVEN
War Clouds Hover

WHEN the *CXF* was brought to a landing beside the great canal just outside the city limits of La-dar, a large crowd had collected to witness the arrival of the traveler's from distant Voris. Two aerocabs drew alongside the great sphere when the outer door of its air-locked entrance was opened, and from the larger of these stepped Torveg himself. The other cab had come for Mirsa and her friends, and was occupied by her father and brother, who welcomed her as affectionately as did Torveg his son. Ronal made haste to present the Princess Ila and the rest of his companions to his father, who straightway offered the hospitality of the palace to all of the Vorisians. He was charmed with Ila, and made a special effort to induce her to make her home in the palace. But she steadfastly refused, though gently, and it was finally arranged that she and Lyris should accompany Mirsa, while Sulor and Andon were to accept the invitation of Torveg and take up their residence in the palace; Barlo drew a breath of satisfaction as he set foot on the soil of his native land; for there had been times when he was certain that he would never see Arin again.

Andites was first to greet Ronal at the palace, and to assure him that vigorous preparations were under way for the defense of La-dar. The city was a turmoil of activity, and the great manufacturing establishments of the entire planet had already been drafted for the turning out of war materials. The scientists of Arin were hard at work on the problems of devising adequate defensive armament and weapons.

"Our great observatories," said Andites, "are constantly on the watch for signs of the approach of the Vorisian vessels. But they have thus far been unable to discover indications that any have yet left Voris. Unfortunately, our telescopes are not of sufficient power to observe objects so small on the surface of the planet itself."

"What measures are being taken to provide defense?"

"There are the long-discarded disintegrating-ray weapons of the police and these are being repaired and charged for use. In addition, a number of large factories are starting work on the production of many more such weapons. This will require some time, of course; and in the interim we are providing for a protective barrier over the roof tops of our great cities."

"A protective barrier? How can this be arranged?"

"By projecting fan-shaped rays of high-frequency vibrations to form above the city a ceiling of pulsations, of such a frequency that the disintegrating rays of the enemy will be neutralized and dissipated before they can reach the surface."

"Can this work be completed in time?"

"That is the great difficulty. Work is being rushed; but it is quite likely that some sections will remain unprotected when the enemy fleet attacks. However, we are doing the best we can under the circumstances, and the invaders will not find Arin entirely defenseless."

"THAT is some consolation, Andites. But what think you of the final outcome?"

The older man gazed solemnly at the young prince. "We can but hope for the best and do everything within our power to fight off the invader. And I fear it is to be a great task," he stated.

"Yes," agreed Ronal gloomily, "and many of our people will lose their lives and much property will be destroyed."

"It makes but little difference," replied Andites, "for the days of our existence are already numbered, regardless of the impending conflict."

"Why, what do you mean?"

"I had not intended to tell you until a year had passed; but this development has altered all our plans, and I may as well inform you now. Ronal, all life on our planet—as well as that on the planet Voris—is doomed to extinction by natural agencies."

"By natural agencies? Surely you do not anticipate a disaster to the solar system—to the universe?"

"Yes—to the solar system. It is inevitable. Already the evidence of approaching calamity may be observed on the planet Borus,* where animal life has developed to no more than a very elementary stage, and where thinking beings do not yet exist. And the same influences now at work on that planet will shortly make their effects known with us. In fact, the changing seasons of our past few centuries give ample warning of the catastrophe to come; though most of our scientists refuse to recognize the symptoms."

Ronal forgot the menace of Olar for the moment in his astonishment. "What sort of a cataclysm is this to be?" he asked.

"All life on Arin and Voris is to perish by freezing. In your studies you have learned of the glacial epochs in the remote past of Arin and Voris. You are aware of the fact that these periods were encountered almost simultaneously by the two bodies and that warm-blooded animal life became extinct at those times. It is likewise known to you that the climate of Arin is far more rigorous than that of Voris; and some of the reasons for this are apparent to you through your study of astronomy. We have studied the atmospheres of the two

---

*The Earth.

bodies, and know their compositions to a nicety; but we have never before discussed the possibilities I am now about to touch upon. The carbon dioxide content of the atmospheres is the vital factor in what, I believe, is soon to take place."

"Carbon dioxide? But Andites, that is so small a proportion of the atmosphere that, surely, it cannot be of such great importance as you imply."

"IT is of tremendous importance. As you know, if it is present in excessive amounts, our lungs become poisoned, and eventually we die. But aside from that, its variations have a pronounced effect on the climate. The atmosphere itself is a blanket which surrounds a planet and prevents excessive heating of its surface by day and extreme cold by night. But the composition of the atmosphere is what determines its efficiency as an insulating blanket. You are well aware of the fact that frosts occur only when the air is clear and of low humidity. That is the reason for the low temperature of Arin as compared to Voris; for our atmosphere contains much less of moisture than does theirs. Water vapor is less susceptible to the long-wavelength heat radiations from the planet than are nitrogen and oxygen, while there is not so much difference in the absorption of the shorter radiations from the sun.

"But carbon dioxide has the same absorbing effect as water vapor and, even though it makes up a small portion of the atmosphere, it has important climatic effects. In other words, a large amount of carbon dioxide in the atmosphere makes for a warm climate; while a deficiency in this constituent causes lower average temperatures. And the point of all this is that, eventually, the atmospheres of Arin and Voris, as of all other planets in the solar system, are to be deprived of their carbon dioxide, and the temperatures will be so greatly reduced as to make life as we know it impossible."

"But Andites, I still do not understand. What is there to rob the planets of their normal amount of carbon dioxide?"

"Again I say, natural causes. I have made an exhaustive study of the matter and have determined that the glacial periods of ancient times were caused by the passing of the entire solar system through a vast gaseous nebula whose composition is such that all carbon dioxide is absorbed from the atmospheres of those bodies where such an envelope is present. And calculations show that the solar system is again to pass through this nebula within a very few hundred years. Of course, you know that the solar system as a whole is traveling through space, in a vast orbit. Therefore, there must be definite circles, during which the same points are passed through again and again. The time is near; and Arin will become frigid, and its canals will freeze solid. Voris will suffer even more severely; for there is much water on that planet and great glaciers will cover its face, crushing all in their path and snuffing out all life immediately."

"If this is true, how futile are our lives, our loves, and our wars! But how soon do you expect this calamity to overtake us? Within the lifetime of the present generation?"

"Perhaps so, my Ronal. It may be five hundred years and it may be several thousand, but surely not longer than that. So, you see, we have not long to remain here, regardless of the success or failure of the armies of Olar."

Ronal considered deeply. "Nevertheless," he said, at last, "I, for one, am not going to worry about this thing at present. Our successors have much time remaining in which to fret about this calamity, but for us there is an immediate danger that must be overcome. And it seems to me that something in your scientific reasoning might be used to our advantage in the coming war."

Andites was taken aback. "Why, what do you mean?" he asked.

"Just this: If carbon dioxide is so important to the life of a planet, why can we not contrive some means of depleting the atmosphere of Voris—now?"

"Why—why—it is an impossible undertaking! Still I am not sure but that you have put a feasible idea in my mind, at that. Let me see now…"

And Andites became lost in thought; Ronal had indeed made a valuable suggestion. To take advantage of natural forces…!

Then there came a great clamor from the council room of the palace, and Ronal promptly forgot his conversation with Andites as he hastened to learn the cause of the commotion.

"What is it?" he asked, when he had pushed his way through the assemblage of excited nobles and reached the side of Torveg.

"My son," replied the monarch of Marida, "it has been reported that the Vorisian fleet is within 1,500,000 miles of Arin. They will be upon us in less than one unit." (two hours)

Ronal paled. He thought of Ila, in a remote section of the city where defenses had not yet been established. "What are the plans of the council?" he shouted, endeavoring to make himself heard through the clamor.

"They demand that you be appointed commander-in-chief of the defense forces of Marida, and that a desperate effort be made to fight off the invaders. It is presumed that they will first strike at La-dar, for this is the seat of our government."

RONAL'S eyes sparkled in eagerness. "Nothing could be more pleasing to me," he exulted. "Where are the engineers in charge of the installation of the protective-ceiling apparatus?"

A cheer came from the assembled council when it was announced that Ronal was assuming command of the defense; and order was soon restored. The engineers were summoned to a private room, where drawings of the fan-ray generators and maps showing the locations of the completed installations were laid before the young prince.

It was apparent that La-dar was but half protected, for the ceiling-ray generators so far constructed covered only the central portion of the city. The outer residential sections were as yet open to attack, but work was being rushed in those districts as rapidly as possible. Again, with a sinking heart, Ronal thought of Ila where she dwelt with Mirsa's people in unprotected territory.

Haste was imperative and Ronal quickly chose the members of his staff and arranged for the installation of portable etherphones, television instruments and thought-projectors on the roof of the palace, where he intended to make his temporary headquarters. By the time these arrangements were completed there came the report that the enemy fleet was over La-dar, fully fifty of the spherical vessels having been sighted at an altitude of 20,000 feet. Darkness had set in; and the faint luminosity overhead told of the operation of the apparatus of the protective ceiling.

The first battle of the war was about to begin.

CHAPTER EIGHT
War!

RONAL'S first command was that all inhabitants of unprotected areas should proceed to those portions of the city where the ceiling of high-frequency vibrations was in operation. He dispatched a special corps to the home of Mirsa to make certain that Princess Ila and all members of the household were conveyed to safety. Then he turned his attention to the details of organization. He called for Andites, but that worthy was nowhere to be found. He sent for Andon and Sulor, and kept them at hand to advise him regarding the armament of the Vorisian fleet. He set a corps of etherphone operators at work obtaining communication with all countries of Arin and checking up on the defense preparations in all quarters.

Ray projectors of large size were set up in the unprotected areas as rapidly as possible, and these were manned by volunteers, most of whom came from the ranks of the young engineers and engineering students. Then came the first attack on La-dar.

Through the hazy glow of the ceiling of vibrations, they could make out the lights of the Vorisian vessels; then came the orange streaks that carried the disintegrating energy from the generators aboard the great spheres. But these rays never reached the city, though the effects of their striking the protective ceiling was tremendous. Night became day from the vivid display of pyrotechnics above them, as the energy of the rays was expended in the atmosphere above the neutralizing vibrations. Electrical storms were ordinarily unknown in Arin, though they were of common occurrence in Voris, where the atmosphere was cloudy during a great portion of the year. But now the inhabitants of La-dar were treated to an electrical storm of terrifying magnitude. Great flashes of blinding light marked each passage of an orange ray, and terrific peals of thunder followed every flash; the air being disintegrated by the expended energy, and the electricity thus liberated immediately bursting forth in terrific lightning flashes. The populace was terrified, but no damage had thus far been accomplished by the enemy.

Then there was a lull in the storm and it seemed that the commanders of the fleet overhead were engaged in consultation. Ronal spoke rapidly into the microphones, when he observed that a few of the lights above were moving in the direction of an outlying section of the city. Evidently the attackers had become aware of the fact that the protecting ceiling covered only a portion of the city, and were sending a squadron of their ships to destroy the undefended sections. Ronal warned the various division commanders and instructed them to get all available ray projectors ready for immediate use.

"Andon," he said, turning to the son of Sulor, "have you had news of Princess Ila and of Mirsa?"

"No, Your Highness. And we are much concerned."

Again Ronal experienced a wave of cold fear for the safety of Ila. He suddenly realized that the daughter of Olar meant very much to him.

An etherphone operator reported a squadron of seven aeroliners equipped with ray projectors and ready to take off. Ronal ordered these aloft to battle the invader in the skies. Then there was a new development, for a pillar of fire suddenly sprang from a district about three miles from the palace; the enemy had started the work of destruction outside the limits of the protecting ceiling. All eyes were turned in the direction of the flare, while Ronal shouted orders into the microphones. The beams of a dozen powerful searchlights sprang into action and the shapes of three of the spherical vessels were made out over the area under attack. Then came the orange pencils of light from below, and one of the huge spheres was hit squarely. A pulsating glow surrounded the vessel, but beyond that nothing occurred. Another pillar of flame spouted from the city at the point beneath the three enemy vessels. Ronal turned inquiring eyes to Andon.

"The hulls of Olar's vessels are constructed from a metal which is impervious to the disintegrating ray," he explained, "and they will be able to continue dropping their incendiary bombs without fear of molestation."

DISCOURAGED, Ronal wrinkled his brow in thought. Then he made a number of etherphone calls in quick succession, obtaining in turn the chiefs of three of the largest metal-working organizations in Marida. His message to each was the same:

"We must immediately provide weapons to hurl high explosives at the enemy ships," he snapped. "Something on the order of the long-range cannon of ancient days. Or, if your engineers can work out means of hurling such explosives by the use of rays of vibrations, so much the better. But we must have the explosives and their detonators, together with a method of firing them in close proximity to the Vorisian vessels."

A crash nearby told of the destruction of one of the aeroliners overhead. Their ray projectors were useless against the enemy craft, and Ronal ordered the remainder of the squadron to return to its base. The entire northeast section of the city was in flames, but the area covered by the ceiling of vibrations was rapidly growing greater as more of the fan-ray generators were placed in service. Occasional flaming patches on the ceiling above them told of the attempts of the enemy to drop their incendiary bombs through the wall of vibrations. But the metals of which these bombs were constructed were completely disintegrated by contact with the remarkable defensive armor.

There came a call from one of the officials to whom Ronal had talked, "We have fifteen cases of high explosive, Your Highness, with detonators attached. Of course, there are yet no means of firing these at the enemy from below; but why not send aerocabs aloft to drop these bombs on their ships from a higher altitude?"

"The very thing. I shall dispatch a squadron of ships at once. Meanwhile you are to proceed as previously ordered."

"We are obtaining some results already, Your Highness. One of our research men claims he has the very motor needed to project the bombs, and will have it in operation in the morning."

"Very good," approved Ronal. "I shall expect to hear from you early tomorrow."

A squadron of speedy aerocabs was dispatched to the manufacturing plant, which was some 20 miles from the city, and Ronal instructed the commander of the squadron regarding the use of the hastily-improvised bombs. Meanwhile, another section of the city had taken fire, and building after building was demolished by the disintegrating rays of the Vorisians. Ronal groaned in his helplessness.

Still there was no word from Ila.

An hour passed, and the destruction in the outlying districts continued. Refugees were pouring into the protected central part of the city, and gradually this area became of larger size. The engineers were laboring heroically and additional fan-ray generators were placed in service in rapid succession. Then, with a concussion that rocked the city, one of the enemy vessels that hovered not a mile from the palace was blown to bits. A ship of the bombing squadron had been the victor!

Another and another of the great spheres followed; each going the way of the first in a burst of incandescent particles that illuminated the countryside for miles around the city. A great roar came up from the triumphant refugees in the upper levels, where they were huddled on the stationary platforms between the moving ways. Then the remainder of the Vorisian fleet took alarm at this turn of affairs and shot skyward, where the aerocars of the Arinians could not follow. A little while later, the astronomical observatory of La-dar reported the hostile fleet as having come to rest at about a hundred miles from the surface, well out of the atmosphere of Arin. The defense had been temporarily successful; but nearly one-fifth of the city of La-dar was destroyed and several thousand of the inhabitants had perished.

With the tension relaxed, Ronal left Olitan, his second in command, at the microphones, while he proceeded to the council chamber where sat Torveg with a number of his ministers.

"Congratulations, my son," spoke the monarch. "You have handled the situation well and all Marida is proud of you."

"You observed all, Sire'?"

"Yes. The television and the news broadcasts have kept us in constant touch with developments. The idea of the explosives was a master stroke. Who would have thought that so ancient a method of warfare would prove so successful in these times'?"

"It was first thought of by Olar," replied Ronal modestly. "I should never have dreamed of it, had not the destruction of Mi-ran been accomplished by similar means. But it seems that it was not expected here by the enemy."

"No," laughed Torveg, "and they hesitated not in retiring."

"But they will return, never fear," replied Ronal, "and, from what Andon and Sulor tell me, I fear we have some surprises awaiting us. Meanwhile, our defenses are rapidly becoming stronger."

There was a commotion at the doorway, and Sulor entered the royal presence. His face was flushed, and he walked unsteadily as he approached the throne.

"WHAT is it, Sulor?" asked Ronal, fear clutching at his heart.

"Lyris," moaned the grief-stricken Keronian. "It is reported that she and the entire household of Mirsa fell victims to one of the bombs of the enemy."

"What?" gasped Ronal. "Then that means that Ila, too— but it cannot be. You are sure it is true?"

"It is only too true, Your Highness, for word was brought to us by the messengers you sent. Even now Andon is returning with one of your men to the point where the bodies were found."

Ronal gazed appealingly at Torveg, who had listened sadly to this recital.

"That such a calamity as this terrible war should come to us is unthinkable," spoke Torveg, "and to think that the beautiful daughter of Olar should be among the first to perish! It is a blow to you, my son, for I perceive that you were fond of this Princess of Keron."

"Father, I loved her." And Ronal turned his head to hide his feelings.

There was silence in the council chamber, save for the dry sobs of Sulor.

Torveg bowed his head in sorrow.

CHAPTER NINE
Dark Days

THAT night there was little sleep for the people of La-dar and, for that matter, for those of all Marida; while, of all the harassed and bereaved, Ronal was probably the most miserable. Throughout the night he remained at the microphones and screens of his headquarters apparatus, listening to the reports of casualties and watching the work of rescue parties that were busy in the devastated sections. And, all through the long night, there came no word from Andon.

When morning dawned the enemy fleet was seen again descending, and Ronal and his staff watched closely in the screen of the high-magnification television apparatus. To their utter surprise, they saw the fifty spherical ships settle to landings on an arid plain of the dry lands some fifteen miles from the city, where they seemed to be planning an encampment. Then they saw that the occupants of the enemy vessels were disembarking, and that huge quantities of structural materials were being carried to the outside. In the circular area surrounded by the ships of the fleet the Vorisians quickly erected a steel tower the sections of which were fitted together with marvelous exactitude and rapidity. They watched in astonishment while a powerful ray projector was hoisted to the top of the tower and fixed in position, with its reflector directed toward the powdery surface of the plain beneath. Heavy cables were carried from the projector to the interiors of several of the vessels; and then they saw that the ray was boring into the surface of the ground and producing an opening of not less than twenty feet in diameter.

"They are excavating for the purpose of providing underground quarters for their fighters!" gasped Ronal, when the intentions of the invaders became evident.

Then he dispatched a squadron of speedy aerocabs with cargos of the newly-manufactured bombs to destroy the tower and as many of the enemy ships as possible. But the Vorisians also were provided with magnifying television apparatus; for it was soon observed that they were aware of the approach of the scouting fleet from La-dar. Immediately, increased activity became apparent, and several pieces of mechanism which had been carried from their vessels were hastily assembled within the circular enclosure formed by the huge spheres. Before Ronal's fleet had arrived on the scene, these new devices began belching forth what appeared to be immense volumes of gas of a faint blue color. The gas billowed upward and outward until it had completely covered the scene, spreading in all directions and rising to a height of about 500 feet. Then it seemed to cohere into a perfectly-formed hemisphere which enclosed entirely the encampment of the enemy; although it did not render them invisible in the screens. The Vorisians bustled about their tasks as before, with no more concern than peaceable workmen engaged in lawful pursuits.

Ronal questioned Sulor regarding the phenomenon, but to no avail; for it was as strange to that Keronian as it was to the Arinians. The prince then put in an etherphone call for Andites but, as before, was unable to reach him. Then came the images of the scouting aeros in the screen, and he watched intently as they circled high above the enemy encampment. A dark object dropped from one of the small ships; when it struck the semi-transparent hemisphere it rebounded (as from a huge inflated balloon) exploding with terrific violence, but harmlessly, high in the air! Another and another followed, as the tiny craft dropped their cargoes in the vain attempt to destroy the work of the Vorisians. Then came the orange rays from the enemy ships, searching the skies for the darting aeros, passing through and out of the protective bubble with ease. Evidently the gaseous bubble would not protect the enemy against the disintegrating beam; but this was not a necessary precaution, since their vessels were constructed of neutralizing materials. And two of Ronal's detail of eight aeros had vanished in the characteristic smoke puffs that followed contact with the orange rays! Defeated, he ordered the remainder of the squadron to return to its base.

Nonplussed over the new developments, Ronal called for a number of scientists with whom he might consult, and he angrily berated the absent Andites for deserting him at such a crucial time.

A flushed and panting individual made his way across the palace roof and approached the prince. It was Andon!

"Your Highness," he blurted forth, "they are not dead!"

"Ila?" thundered Ronal, his spirits rising with the hope conveyed by the words. And Sulor grasped his son tightly by the arms.

"Lyris; our princess; Mirsa!" sputtered Andon. "They are now together in the Royal Hospital. But you must not be too hopeful, for all three are in a state of suspended animation that baffles the physicians. They may never recover."

Ronal waited to hear no more, but obtained immediate contact with the hospital.

"Melis," he asked of the physician in charge, "exactly what is the condition of Princess Ila and her companions? I must know."

"It is a peculiar case, Your Highness," came the measured reply. "To all appearances the three women are dead, as are the father and brother of Mirsa. There is no respiration; no pulse; no organs are functioning, except the nervous systems. It is only by means of the cellexciter apparatus that we have been able to determine that they are not really dead. And there are many more such in La-dar. The hospitals are filling rapidly with the poor creatures. It is the effect of some gas that the enemy used in the raid."

"Will they recover?"

"It is highly problematical, Your Highness. There are no available means of counteracting the effects of this strange poison, but our physiologists are laboring on the problem. If we but knew the nature of the gas, it might be simpler."

"But we do not, Melis." And Ronal turned from the instrument in discouragement.

THEN he conceived an idea, and spoke rapidly to Andon, who was now engaged in telling the story to his father. "Andon," he said, "if a gas has caused this condition of our loved ones, there must be some samples of it on the *CXF*. They will be invaluable to our scientists, in saving lives. Go—go quickly to the ship and obtain one of each of the various types of bombs stored in her compartments. The ship is unharmed; for it was within the area of the protective ceiling."

Andon's face lighted at the words and Sulor raised his head in renewed hope. "I go, Your Highness," exclaimed the young Keronian, and he hastened from their presence. "Your Highness," spoke up Olitan, from his position at the screen, "here is another marvel that the enemy is accomplishing."

The view in the screen was changed but little. The huge bubble still covered the encampment of the Vorisians. But there now showed a great pit, which had been excavated close to the vertical shaft under the ray projector tower. The pit was round, about a hundred feet in diameter, and half that depth. A number of portable ray projectors had been used in hollowing it out. And, most remarkable of all, from two huge tanks which had been erected at its rim there poured streams of sparkling water. The pit was rapidly filling to form a small artificial lake.

"Where can they have obtained the water?" ejaculated Ronal.

"They are producing it synthetically, Your Highness," was the solemn reply of Olitan.

Looking more closely, Ronal saw that what he said was true. A disintegrating apparatus was at work, arranging the disrupted atoms into collectors where the protons and electrons were united to form new elements—oxygen and hydrogen. The collecting tanks were connected to a huge retort, which discharged into the tanks at the shore of the pond. The Vorisians were combining the two gases in the proportion of one part of oxygen and two parts of hydrogen, thus producing pure water for their consumption, where none had been available in the dry lands of Arin! This was a process unknown to the Arinians; there were some things for them to learn from the crafty scientist of Voris.

Late that afternoon, the second fleet of fifty vessels arrived and another attack was made on La-dar. This was highly unsuccessful, for the protecting ceiling was now complete. But the counter-attack of Ronal's aeros, of which there were now twenty-five, equipped with ray projectors and high-explosive bombs, was likewise unsuccessful. The second fleet from Voris retreated quickly to the protection of the bubble in the dry lands; then the first departed, leaving behind nearly ten thousand fighting men of Voris, who kept doggedly at whatever devilish work they were engaged, below the surface of the dry lands.

DAY after day the enemy continued with their labors, and each attack of Ronal's forces showed more clearly to the defenders how impregnable was their position. There were now about 20,000 Vorisians at work and, with alternate trips of the two fleets, it was expected that this number would be augmented by another 10,000 every twelve days. Undoubtedly, they were tunneling beneath the surface with the intention of coming up under the city of La-dar where the protective ceiling would be of no avail.

Scouts were repeatedly sent out under cover of darkness to learn what they might of the nature of the protective bubble of the Vorisians and of their workings within its confines. But these scouts never returned to tell of their experiences.

Transmitting beams had been perfected, to hurl the high-explosive bombs at the enemy; and these were tried out in vain against that impenetrable bubble in the dry lands. Then came the return of the enemy fleet with another ten thousand fighters; and a cloud of aeros went out to meet them, carrying the new beam generators and a plentiful supply of bombs. But once more the forces of Arin failed; for now each of the enemy's spherical ships was enclosed by its own gas envelope, and the protection wall as complete as that of the bubble surrounding the encampment. The reinforcements were landed without the loss of a single vessel of Voris, while the Arinians lost many aeros and one hundred and eighty men. The people of La-dar became panicky, and their fear was communicated to the far corners of Arin through the reports of the news broadcasts.

Ronal held daily consultations with the foremost scientists of the realm. Many schemes for overcoming the enemy were proposed and, one after another, rejected as impracticable. The prince missed his old friend and tutor acutely during this period, and began to fear for his safety.

Then, too, there was Ila; and Ronal's heart ached when he thought of her, so white and still in her hospital bed. All efforts to analyze the gases obtained from the *CXF* by Andon were fruitless. And, each day, the bodies of the totally paralyzed victims grew less responsive to the cell exciters. It was generally conceded that the Princess Ila, like some four hundred other patients who were in similar condition, had little chance of recovery.

Ronal's spirits approached the nadir of despair and, were it not for the comfortings of wise old Torveg, he would have been tempted to give up in hopelessness.

CHAPTER TEN
The Return of Andites

IN La-dar there were now more than fifty thousand men and women trained in the use of ray pistols and the heavier projectors, which appeared to be the most effective weapons for use in hand-to-hand conflict. And it became certain that the war was to develop into a series of such engagements. Scouts reported that more than a hundred thousand Vorisians were now in Arin; and three more of the bubble-protected strongholds had been established in widely-separated portions of the planet. In each case the enemy's encampment was located within a few miles of the capital city of a great province, and all efforts of the Arinians failed to rout the Vorisians from their positions. Additional space fliers had been constructed in Voris; and the ranks of the invaders were being swelled at the rate of ten thousand every five days. All small communities throughout the globe were abandoned, their inhabitants flocking to the larger cities where the defenses were being organized. The overcrowding which resulted caused great hardship, and further served to increase the demoralization of the frightened masses of the populace.

In anticipation of an underground attack on La-dar, Ronal had ordered the construction of defenses far beneath the ground level. Hundreds of engineers were at work with their boring rays, honeycombing the ground with tunnels and caverns where defensive armor and huge beam generators were set up. A constant vigil was maintained by means of sound detectors which would indicate the close approach of enemy workings; and it was planned to meet them when their tunnels were broken through and to engage them in a hand-to-hand struggle.

But, faced by an endless supply of reinforcements arriving from Voris, it was apparent that the war was to be long drawn out. For the population of Voris was more than five times as great as that of Arin; and Olar had an almost unlimited number of fighters to draw upon.

Meanwhile, unknown to Ronal, old Andites, keeping constantly informed of the state of affairs by means of his broadcast and television receivers, was hard at work in his secret laboratory in one of the long unused sublevels of La-dar. Nearly three months had passed since the first battle of the war; and long hours of labor and lack of sleep had caused a great change in the old savant. He was pitifully thin and haggard. But his mind was keener than ever, and today there was a gleam of satisfaction in his tired gray eyes.

"Ah, at last," he muttered, as he completed the final adjustments of a mechanism that reposed on one of his work benches. "I have discovered the secret, Arin is saved—until the great cold."

HIS fingers trembled as he inserted a small lump of clay in a tiny crucible, which he placed on a small platform. Above this platform was a series of vacuum tubes, each of a different shape, and each connected to the apparatus by many wires of large diameter. He closed a switch, and the musical hum of a powerful dynamo machine beneath the table responded. Then he manipulated a number of dials on the face of the apparatus and, when these were adjusted to his satisfaction, he pressed a button which lighted the many tubes over the little crucible. From each tube there shot a ray of different character, some red, some blue, some of dazzling whiteness. All rays converged on the tiny lump of clay, and a wisp of smoke curled upward from the container. Then there was a roar as of a terrific windstorm within the confines of the crucible; and Andites laughed aloud in his glee. He opened the main switch and the dynamo stopped, the light of the several tubes fading. But the roar in the crucible continued and, with a thick sheet of asbestos held before him to protect his body from the intense heat, Andites stepped to the platform and gazed into the miniature inferno he had created.

The tiny lump of clay had become a whirling fury of dazzling brightness and, as it spun madly within the crucible, its radiations produced strange effects in the large room which was Andites' laboratory. The walls trembled and the very air pulsated to the intense energy of the minute sphere of tortured matter. The walls of the crucible became incandescent and the radiated heat was so intense that Andites retreated to the far wall of the room. Then, as the roar of the energy mounted to a volume that nearly shattered his ear drums, the crucible and its demoniac contents vanished in a puff of flame and with a jar that shook the foundations of the building. Andites gazed spellbound at the empty platform for a moment, then rushed from the room.

He hastened to his living quarters and removed his soiled clothing. A cold mist shower put new strength in his tired body, and he attired himself carefully for the important visit to the palace. He was consumed with eagerness to impart his astounding news to Ronal, and lost no time in making his way to the military headquarters of the young prince.

"Andites!" exclaimed Ronal, when he looked up from one of the television screens and encountered the gaze of his friend. "I had just about given you up as lost. But truly, it is good to see you once more!"

And, before the eyes of his astonished staff, the young prince leaped to his feet and threw his arms around the body of the older man, hugging him enthusiastically as he had been wont to do when a mere lad.

"It is likewise good to see you, my Ronal." The eyes of Andites were softened and happy, as he looked into those of the prince.

"Where have you been, my Andites? And what have you been doing?"

"I have been at work in my hidden laboratory, my lad. And a momentous discovery has resulted—a discovery that will rid Arin of the menace of Voris!"

"You mean...?"

But before Andites could reply there came an interruption. The great alarm siren of the palace let forth its wail of warning and all eyes turned to the viewing screens that pictured the underground defenses of La-dar. The enemy had broken through!

INSTANTLY Ronal gave his every attention to the microphones, and Andites stood proudly by as the young commander barked his orders into the instruments. Ten thousand fresh troops of La-dar were converging at the point where the tunnel of the Vorisians had entered their own workings. The scene in the viewing screen was one of indescribable confusion, as hundreds of fighting men crowded into a cavern which became so closely packed that the ray pistols were almost useless. Hand-to-hand conflicts developed, and the noise of the melee, as it came through the amplifiers, was deafening. Then a puff of smoke showed in the cavern, and for a few moments all sight was obscured, though the shouting of the combatants continued unabated. Then there was an ominous stillness and slowly the smoke cleared away, drifting leisurely through connecting tunnels toward the outer air. And what a sight met the eyes of the observers when they were again able to discern the objects in the cavern! The fighters of La-dar were stretched lifeless; and only then was it seen that the Vorisians wore small gas masks that covered mouth and nose and thus saved them from what lethal gas they had released.

Ronal warned his lieutenants immediately, and four companies were directed to advance along connecting tunnels, behind the armor of neutralizing metals which had been provided on their high-power movable ray projectors. Soon there came the flash of a beam that cut a swath through the massed troops of Olar, and accounted for a full hundred of them before they were able to erect their own protective screens. Then, proceeding behind the insulating covers, companies of the invaders streamed into the connecting tunnels and advanced on the waiting Arinians.

One of Ronal's aides was plotting a line on a chart and he called the attention of the prince to what he had done.

"See this, Your Highness," he said. "This is the location of the cavern, and the enemy's tunnel extends in this direction toward their headquarters in the dry lands."

Ronal examined the chart and wrinkled his brow in thought. "The elevation at their headquarters?" he asked.

"Minus twelve feet, Your Highness."

"And of the lower levels of La-dar?"

"Plus fifteen feet. That is, not counting on the depth of the recent workings."

"Good!" And Ronal became a whirlwind of energy.

HE dispatched a corps of engineers to the great canal at the point where the enemy tunnel crossed its broad width. Rapidly he issued instructions for them to open a huge gap through the intervening ground with their ray projectors. Then he commanded the troops under the city to retreat slowly, using every effort to keep protected and to hold back the advancing enemy as long as possible. Ray projectors were to be kept in constant action to beat back the gas fumes as they were released from the Vorisian bombs. The caverns and tunnels were filled with the advancing hordes of Olar and they were pressing steadily forward, searing tunnel walls and floors with the heavy discharges of their disintegrators. On either side it was certain death for a fighter to expose any portion of his body beyond the edges of the screens. And here and there the gas gained headway, leaving always in its wake a heap of lifeless Arinians. The gas masks of La-dar proved useless against these strange vapors, while those of the Vorisians seemed effective in protecting their wearers against all gases used by the defenders.

Ronal manipulated the controls of the television, and on the screen appeared the view of the great canal where his engineers were at work. Great clouds of steam rose from the dark waters as the projectors bored deeply into the bed of the canal. Then there was a shout from the workers and the steam clouds drifted away, leaving a whirling eddy in the waters whence they had emanated. The great canal was pouring into the tunnel below.

There was consternation in the enemy's ranks when the water came rushing in upon them, and those on the near side of the point of influx were of necessity compelled to continue their advance toward the city. Those on the far side beat a hasty retreat in the direction of their headquarters in the dry lands, being forced, eventually, to the surface by the rising waters.

Now the defenders were putting up a terrific resistance to the invaders, who found themselves between the advancing waters and the suddenly invincible Arinians. As the Vorisians were forced into the higher levels under the city, they were flanked by company after company of Ronal's troops, who poured the deadly rays of their disintegrators into the struggling invaders from the several tunnel mouths that entered at many points behind protective screens.

Ronal sent a fleet of aeros to the enemy headquarters in the dry lands; and these hovered expectantly over the great bubble, keeping close watch on the Vorisians as they poured in great numbers from the shaft mouth and retreated to their spherical vessels. Then came the waters, gushing from the mouth of the pit like a geyser. The generators of the mysterious bubble ceased functioning as they were flooded. Then came a rain of high explosives from the vessels of Arin, and six or seven of the huge spheres were blasted out of existence. But the rest had managed to surround themselves with the protective gas; and these rose rapidly to attack the Arinian fleet, bringing about the destruction of fully twenty of the smaller craft before a retreat could be organized.

The battle beneath the city still raged furiously, but the defenders were emerging victorious. Ronal turned happily to face the solemn eyes of Andites. He exulted openly.

"It was a great idea, my Ronal," approved Andites, "but it is no more than a temporary setback to the enemy. Olar can outnumber us by five to one and he has but begun his campaign."

"True," admitted Ronal. And his face fell. "But how are we to outmaneuver the tyrant?"

"By destroying the planet Voris," whispered Andites.

"Destroying it? Annihilating an entire planet?"

"Exactly."

"Can this be done?"

"It can. The discovery of which I spoke provides the means."

Ronal gazed wonderingly into the honest eyes of Andites, unmindful of the jubilant reports of victory which were coming in from his various lieutenants. But he did not forget to order the canal bottom repaired, to conserve the precious water.

CHAPTER ELEVEN
Reverses

THE battle beneath La-dar raged for three days. No quarter was asked and none given; and eventually the last remnants of the invaders were exterminated. But it was at terrible cost to the defenders, for not less than twenty thousand casualties were counted. There was mourning throughout all Marida, and jubilation over the victory was not to be thought of.

The enemy had established a new base for operations on the other side of La-dar; not more than five miles from the city limits, where no canal intervened to permit of a repetition of the first repulse. In making this move, the Vorisians were harried and attacked by hundreds of the newly equipped vessels of Marida, and they lost one of their huge spheres during these encounters. But the new headquarters was successfully established and eleven of the Arinian vessels and their crews were destroyed.

Andites was given a free hand in the carrying out of his scheme, and was laboring incessantly with the research engineers of several of the large manufacturing corporations. Crates of heavy machinery began to arrive at the observatory of La-dar within five days of the time of starting work, and the erection of the new apparatus went forward with unprecedented speed.

The air was filled with urgent messages from the high-power radio transmitters of the enemy, but these were unintelligible to the people of Arin; for it had not been found possible to decipher the complex code. Neither was it possible to rectify the distorted modulation of the low-power etherphones and thought-projectors used by the Vorisians for carrying on their inter-headquarters communications, though Andon had used the apparatus of the *CXF* in his efforts to do this. The characteristics of the distorting mechanism had been altered after the loss of the *CXF*, in anticipation of just such attempts by the people of Arin.

Ronal spent much time at the hospital in consultation with the physicians and at the bedside of Ila. Of the four hundred patients originally under observation, more than three hundred had passed from the state of suspended animation into the decay that means death. But Ila was one of the few who still maintained evidence of susceptibility to cell-excitation, and, though she gave the appearance of a lifeless marble statue of divine beauty, there was still the possibility that she might eventually be saved. If only the scientists could determine the exact nature of this peculiar affliction. Then, thought Ronal, they would be in a position to determine a means of effecting a cure. He must talk to Andites about the matter. His hopes rose at the thought, but were dashed when he gazed at the still form of the daughter of Olar. Surely there was no hope; when already more than three-fourths of the victims had perished. And strange it was that he, who had never interested himself in the fair sex, was so deeply and hopelessly enamored of this beautiful Princess of Keron. Stranger still, that he should be planning the destruction of her home planet, her father's death.

THEN came news of the direst disaster of the war. Pulans, the magnificent capital city of Orsto, was occupied by the enemy. Pulans, second only to La-dar, a mass of ruins, with eighty thousand of its inhabitants slain! The remaining four million or more of its people were placed in a degrading subjection to the tyrant of Kir! Ronal ground his teeth in futile rage. And, every two or three days now, fresh troops arrived from Voris; there were now estimated to be more than two hundred of the spherical space cars making regular round trips between the two planets. Each day the activities of the enemy increased in magnitude and ferocity. Truly, the one course left open for the salvation of Arin was the utter destruction of Voris and its conquest-mad millions.

Torveg seemed to age many years in those terrible days, during which the victories of the armies of Olar became more and more widespread and devastating. He trembled at thought of the fate of the twelve million inhabitants of Ladar; for he realized that the Vorisians would be successful in overpowering their inadequate defenses. He wept over the reports of indignities heaped upon the people of Pulans; over the wanton destruction of priceless works of art; over murder and rapine. Five other large cities of Arin, having populations of between three and four millions each, were in imminent danger of occupation by the relentless foe. Things looked very dark indeed for his beloved subjects. He refused to be comforted by the assurances of Ronal that Andites was working out their salvation in the laboratories and factories of Marida. Not a scientist at heart, he was unable to appreciate the possibilities inherent in a new discovery.

Andon and Sulor were assisting Andites, and labored day and night in the effort to hasten the destruction of Olar. They were vengeful and bitter, and the long hours of deep concentration seemed to aid in relieving somewhat their sorrow over the fate of Lyris. They had long since given up hope of her recovery, though the beloved wife and mother remained in about the same condition as did the Princess Ila.

IN the great dome room of the observatory, Andites was completing the final adjustment of the complicated apparatus that had been installed near the supporting pillar of the huge reflector. He smiled with satisfaction when he found that all was in excellent working order. The many careful workmen who had by their united efforts made possible this triumph of engineering had done their work well. The time was at hand!

Andites stepped to the etherphone and quickly obtained a connection with the palace.

"Ronal," he said, exultantly, when the voice of his beloved prince responded to the call. "All is in readiness. This is the night of the great accomplishment. Come to the observatory at once and bring Torveg with you."

"The power connections are complete?"

"They are, my Ronal. The entire generating capacity of Marida has been linked together in one great superpower system. We have the power of more than nine billion men available."

"You are certain of success, Andites?"

"Positively. If this scheme fails, then I would be willing to admit that mathematics and its allied sciences are fallible and natural laws are disproved. No, my Ronal, there is no possibility of failure."

"I trust that you are correct. And I have no cause to doubt you now, my Andites, for you have never spoken anything but truth. We will proceed to the observatory at once."

It was just before midnight, and Voris shone faintly, high in the heavens. The great reflecting telescope was trained on the planet, and the clock in its massive pedestal kept the orb in constant view. Andites peered earnestly into the eyepiece and made a slight adjustment to center the body exactly with the cross-hairs. He stepped to the many-paneled switchboard and checked the multitude of feeder switches where the incoming power beams, conveyed their vast supply of energy to the main busses. All was in order. He rubbed his palms together in an anticipatory excitement. He gazed upward to where the outer end of the telescope pointed toward the broad open slit in the dome, and he thought grimly of the power that was to spout forth from the massive sixty-foot iridium ring that surrounded its tip. No human being in all Arin, save only Andites, knew what enormous forces were to be released when the main control of his apparatus was closed.

"WE have arrived, Andites." The voice of Ronal greeted him close by, and he turned to observe that the royal party included a number of distinguished personages, in addition to Torveg and the young prince.

"You are welcome, Highness." And Andites, with a smile, stood stiffly at attention.

Torveg glanced nervously about him at the gleaming contrivances that seemed to lurk everywhere in the shadows of the immense dome room. "Do I understand, Andites," he asked, "that you believe this new mechanism of yours will destroy the planet Voris?"

"That is correct, Your Majesty. And I shall demonstrate it in a very few minutes."

"If it works—if it works," muttered Torveg incredulously, "our people are saved. For the quarter-million Vorisians now in Arin will perforce surrender. Their home destroyed, they will have no source of supplies, no further reinforcements. The radium* from which their energies are obtained will run short and there will be no means of replenishing the supply. Yes—they must surrender—yet it seems a pity that Voris, once the home of a magnificent civilization, should be utterly destroyed because of the sins of its present inhabitants."

---

*In the thought message the expression conveyed was "the metal of fiery power that constantly loses its substance."

The great ruler of all Arin shook his head solemnly. But Ronal and the nobles of his court voiced strenuous objection. It was no time to waste maudlin pity on an enemy who threatened the very existence of their own civilization. Andites chuckled, as he advanced to the lower end of the telescope and attached a shining cylinder to its eyepiece. Then he pressed a button and the dome room was in darkness save for the brilliance of the image of Voris projected through the metal cylinder to the surface of a vertical screen. A deathly stillness fell over everything, a silence broken only by the sound of Andites' feet as he stepped to the switchboard and pulled a lever that clanked ominously as it swung to its closed position.

On the screen Voris was pictured as a brilliant orb some six feet in diameter, its oceans and continents standing forth in bold relief. But the eyes of the observers were drawn skyward by the sound of a throbbing roar which was set up by the throwing of the main switch—a roar that told of more than a billion and a quarter horse-powers of energy projected into space. Through the slit of the dome they could see a pulsating violet beam that extended far into the blackness of the heavens and in the direction of Voris.

The voice of Andites came hoarsely as he raised it to make himself heard over the now deafening uproar:

"The beam which has set forth on its long journey to Voris will reach there in fifteen minutes. It carries tremendous energy that will penetrate to the vitals of the planet, and there set up a progressive atomic disintegration that will accomplish our purpose. This is the secret of the new apparatus. The disintegration is internal, not external, as in the case of our regular disintegrator rays. These could not be used; for the energy required would be unattainable. But with the atoms in the heart of the planet once disrupted, they will continue their work of destruction without further aid.

Being confined under tremendous pressure, the exploding of one atom will set off the next adjacent one, then the next, *ad infinitum.* The planet's internal heat will increase so terrifically, and so rapidly, that the crust will be unable to withstand the pressure; an explosion of enormous magnitude will result."

THEY watched breathlessly—endlessly, it seemed. "The beam is at work," Andites eventually announced.

Another period of waiting. The clear image of Voris as seen on the screen did not alter in the slightest degree. Minutes passed; minutes that seemed like hours. Then a huge crack appeared across the surface. Another and another followed in quick succession, and the watchers gasped as the physical contours of the continents underwent rapid metamorphosis. Dense clouds of steam belched forth from the fissures which soon widened to yawning chasms. The entire planet was obscured by the billowing clouds of vapor. Then came a burst of vivid flame from out the swirling whiteness, and great sections of the globe were flung off in all directions, heated to a dazzling incandescence by the fury from within. Wabbling uncertainly, these masses went hurtling off into space. Another huge burst of flame—more flying fragments—and Voris was no more.

Then came that reaction Andites had anticipated, but that brought angst to the watchers and spread terror across Arin. The ground shook. Roaring winds howled with demoniac fury. The heavens spun round crazily and, in the space of a few minutes, the sun rose—fully four hours ahead of time!

The unexpected rays of the morning sun, flashing suddenly through the slit of the dome, fell across the awed group near the greater reflector. In their midst, on the hard floor, knelt Torveg, tears streaming down his furrowed cheeks. In faltering and well-nigh incoherent whispers, now audible in the sudden stillness, he gave thanks to his Maker.

CHAPTER TWELVE
Peace

LONG after the royal visitors had left the observatory, Andites remained at the telescope with one of the staff astronomers. Many observations were made and much data compiled regarding the new order of things in the solar system. Voris was no more, and its fragments had gone to make up a great number of new small bodies, each with its own independent orbit. Of these there were at least eight hundred, and possibly as many as a thousand. The disturbance to the solar system occasioned by the redistribution of forces was slight, though its effects had seemed tremendous to the lay populace—Arin was shifted from its normal orbit by but a few thousand miles. The inclination of its equator to the plane of its orbit had been altered not more than one degree. But the momentary resultant of the many changing forces had been so terrific as to turn the planet on its axis almost ninety degrees in the direction of rotation, thus accomplishing in a very few minutes what ordinarily took place in one-sixth of a day, and thereby causing the sun to rise four hours sooner than usual on that eventful morning. The rate of rotation seemed not to have permanently altered, however; so it was not expected that any great change would be experienced in climate or in other physical conditions. But one set of observations caused Andites to ponder very deeply, and he suddenly left his companion and hastened to the palace to communicate to Ronal his startling conclusions.

Passing through the upper ways, he found that confusion reigned throughout La-dar, though the public news broadcasts blared forth reassuring announcements at each intersection.

"Ronal," he stated mysteriously, when he had been admitted to the chambers of the young prince, "this disturbance in our solar system has saved us from the greatest disaster of all, or at least postponed it for many, many centuries."

"Why, what mean you, Andites?"

"The great cold that I told you was coming. The path of the solar system through interstellar space has been altered—very slightly, it is true, but still sufficiently so that we shall miss the first great gaseous nebula that was to rob us of our carbon dioxide."

"Then Arin is to survive indefinitely after all?"

"Not indefinitely, but the time of the great cold will be greatly delayed until a second and larger nebula must be encountered."

Ronal smiled in spite of himself. "That should give us little concern at the present moment, my Andites," he chuckled. "You and I will long since have been forgotten when that time comes."

"True!" Andites wagged his head sagely. "But there is still an important problem to be considered for the benefit of future generations."

A PAGE interrupted their conversation, handing a scroll to the young prince.

"Hm," muttered Ronal, when he had glanced over the writing. "Malick, commander of the forces of Olar, is suing for peace. One of their bases was destroyed by earthquake at the time Voris exploded. One hundred and ten vessels of his fleet were destroyed with the planet, for they had just arrived there from Arin. Supplies are already low in their encampments; they must yield."

"It is as we expected. They are cowards at heart. And do you intend to spare them?"

"What else can we do? We are compassionate beings and must show mercy, else we ourselves become miserable. But they will make good laborers in the mines and factories. Yes, I shall spare them."

Ronal paced the floor in a state of intense feeling, and Andites regarded him with understanding eyes. "You will send word at once?" he inquired.

"Malick awaits my reply in the open square atop the palace. I go to him immediately."

And with these words he strode from the room and made for the lift. Andites following him closely.

Awaiting his coming was a delegation comprising not less than twenty Vorisians, the figure of the commander conspicuous by his ostentatious display of medals and other decorations. And a thoroughly cowed and dejected lot these survivors were.

"Your Highness," inquired Malick, "has read the scroll?"

"I have." This from Ronal in his most haughty and condescending manner.

"You will offer terms of peace?"

"Yes, but mark you, Malick, they will be hard. We of Arin are soft-hearted, but we must steel ourselves to deal properly with foes such as the Vorisians have proved themselves to be. We did not make this war, but we have ended it; and we propose to settle with your invading armies as we see fit. A truce is hereby declared until suitable papers can be drawn up and signed. Meanwhile you are to surrender your arms, your vessels, and the secrets of the many gases and other offensive means you have used against us. My staff will appoint companies of our troops to take over these munitions and guard your encampments. Your men's lives are to be spared, miserable as they are, and they will be supplied with food and other necessities. But these must be earned by honest toil in a manner we shall later prescribe. That is all, for the present."

HE turned to leave the presence of the delegation of Vorisians, but stopped in his tracks as his eyes rested on an emblem worn by one of their number, a court physician of high standing. Ronal was seized with a sudden idea. He rushed to the astonished Keronian and grasped him roughly by the arm.

"You are a physician?" he barked.

"I am." The startled medical man winced under the pressure of Ronal's powerful fingers.

"You are acquainted with the effects of the gas that causes a state of suspended animation and eventually results in death?"

"Yes."

"You are able to cure victims of this gas?"

"In certain cases. That is, where the action has not been allowed to persist too long a period of time."

"Come with me!" Ronal jerked him unceremoniously from the midst of his companions and hurried him to the waiting elevator. In a few moments they were on their way to the hospital where lay Ila the beautiful, orphaned daughter of Olar.

*   *   *

"It is too late," whispered Melis, when questioned by Ronal at the door of the room occupied by Ila, Lyris and Mirsa. "The Princess has crossed the border line. Her body is now being prepared for interment."

The young prince went ghastly white and he turned savagely on Tilon, the Keronian physician who backed away in awe. "You hear that?" shouted Ronal. "It is the Princess Ila they say has died—Ila the beautiful, killed by the hand of Olar, as was her poor mother! By the imps of the dry lands, I'll kill you with my bare hands unless you bring her back!"

"Ila!" gasped Tilon, his face as white as Ronal's and his limbs trembling. "She, a victim of the Bor gas! But perhaps your physicians do not know. There may be hope. Where is she?"

Quickly he became the alert professional man, and quickly he followed Melis into the supposed room of death.

Ronal was left to pace the halls in an agony of hope and fear. He was in need of medical attention himself, for his nerves were near the breaking point. During many trying days he had obtained little or no sleep, and the climax had been followed by a reaction that threatened to break even his iron constitution. A cold sweat broke forth on his forehead, and he moaned in anguish of body and mind as he kept vigil.

Would they never finish? It seemed that hours of deathly stillness had already passed. And still there was no sound from behind that spotlessly white steel door. He would keep his word and throttle the life out of the pampered doctor from Olar's court. Yes, a thousand Keronian warriors should pay the penalty if Ila had indeed passed on! He would break his word to Malick—they were a vile, worthless lot, anyway; and the lives of a million of them were not worth the wee finger of Ila's hand. The door opened, and Ronal stopped in his pacing as if halted by the discharge of a ray pistol. Melis approached him. Was he smiling or dejected? Name of the imps, he was smiling! Ronal grasped him by the shoulders and shook him roughly.

"Tell me! Tell me!" he exclaimed, "will she recover?"

"She will recover, Your Highness. But, if it please you, I wish to be released. There are still thirty of our people who might be saved—now that we have the method."

"To be sure. To be sure." Dazedly, Ronal released his grip and watched the busy physician hurry into the adjoining room. Then he stepped to the door of Ila's room and cautiously peered within. Tilon was bending over the figure of Lyris, who lay on the adjoining bed. Ila he saw, lay white and quiescent beneath her own snowy covers. He advanced quietly to her side.

Wonder of wonders, the long lashes lifted! The great eyes opened wide. The princess recognized him. She smiled; a smile so sweet and tender that Ronal dropped to his knees at her bedside and gazed and gazed in awed thankfulness.

"You are able to speak?" he whispered.

"A little, my prince," she replied weakly. "How long have I been ill?"

"Many days, dear. But now you are coming back. You are to be well once more. And never again shall you leave the side of Ronal."

"The war?"

"Is over. But you must not think of that now. You must think only of getting your strength back."

"Voris was defeated?"

"Voris has been completely destroyed, sweetheart. There is nothing more to fear."

A wave of color mantled the exquisitely-chiseled features as Ila heard the word of endearment. At the moment she looked as if she had never been ill a day in her life. Suddenly she moved her fingers, reached for his hand.

"You love me?" she asked.

"More than my life. It is too much to hope that you likewise love me."

Her eyes answered him. Then she sighed and, pressing his hand tightly, fell into a natural sleep. He stood erect and tiptoed softly to the side of Tilon, who looked up at his approach.

"Thank you, Tilon," he said. "You have given Ila back to me. I love her, you know."

"Hm," grunted the unimpressed Keronian. "Many loved her in Voris. But she would have none of them. I suppose you are to be congratulated. Anyway, I am glad to save them all. The others also will recover."

And he went about his business unconcernedly. Ronal stared at him in amazement. It seemed to him at that moment that the entire universe should be singing to the tune that was in his own heart. He gazed once more at the beloved features of the princess, then dashed madly for the lift. He must break the glad news at once to Torveg, to Andites, to Barlo! And the happiness that was to come to Andon and Sulor!

There was now no need of a physician for Ronal. His cure was complete.

EPILOGUE

HERE ended the Martian "thought book" which so appealed to the author. Others of these remarkable histories, which came to us after ages of time, tell of the wise rule of Ronal after the death of Torveg, and of the great love he bore his consort, Ila the beautiful. They tell of succeeding generations and the peace and prosperity that reigned throughout Arin to the end, when the great cold eventually came in accordance with the predictions of Andites. But, in all this collection of ancient information, there is no story so appealing as that of the two young people of royal blood whose lives were so closely associated with the events of that last great war; a war responsible for the removal of a planet from our solar system and the substitution of the asteroids which were formed from its fragments.

That the existence of warm-blooded animal life on the planet Mars, was snuffed out with the coming of the "great cold" is clearly evidenced by the last of the "thought books" to be enclosed with the machines which make them intelligible to us today. It was likewise proved by the condition of the fossil remains unearthed by the two scientists, Moody and Bedworth, and now on view in the International Museum atop the transoceanic air stage in Washington. That such life has never since inhabited the planet is ascribed to the scarcity of water. Knowing, as we now do, that the sea is the mother of all life, it is easy to understand that there would be little opportunity for a new form of life to originate after the great cold, since no seas exist.

To those who are interested in the family life of the people of Arin during the days of Ronal and Ila, it is recommended that Moody's latest book be examined from cover to cover. It is not to be supposed that the average reader will care to wade through the lengthy technical wording; but there are many illustrations of the finest sort that picture clearly the remains of household articles, the moving ways of the cities, close-ups of the great canals, and other scenes of interest pictured exactly as found by those two daring scientists. These illustrations are reproductions of photographs taken during their stay on the dead planet and serve to show many phases of the lives of those ancients who looked, lived, loved and acted much as we do today, but who were so greatly in advance of us in scientific attainment.

On a clear night, when Mars is close to Earth, you might take a trip to one of the large observatories and beg for a peep through its modern super-telescope. If you are so fortunate as to obtain a good view, you will see for yourself many of the broad canals that cover the surface, and may even distinguish the ruins of La-dar beside the canal which our astronomers have called Pierius.

Or, if of venturesome disposition, you might even consider the offer of Bedworth recently made through our own news broadcasts. He and Moody, it will be remembered, have obtained the necessary financial backing, and started the construction of a spherical space flier similar to those of the people of Voris. This vessel is now completed, and they will allow fifty able-bodied Americans to accompany them on a three-year trip to Mars. This is undoubtedly a wonderful chance; and there may be some of you who are sufficiently interested to take advantage of the offer and thereby embark on a glorious adventure.

The author, however, is inclined to prefer the "'thought books" as a source of entertainment and information. Possibly a bit of the cautious nature of old Torveg has been passed along through the medium of those slender wires. At any rate, even amidst the wonders of America in 1980, we, too, are doubtful of the high state of perfection of some of these "new-fangled" inventions—at least to such a degree that we have no desire to make the long voyage to Arin.

THE END

THIS IS NOT A WINTER WONDERLAND!

Stephen Reynard Dunraven was a talented amateur Paleontologist on a geological dig in the wilds of Mexico. While crawling around inside ancient ruins, Dunraven discovered that an ancient civilization had existed before our own, one that had been destroyed by what was commonly known as "the fifth ice age." But Dunraven had also discovered an ancient scientific calendar, a calendar that indicated when the next devastating ice age would shake the world. If true, Dunraven knew that glaciers from either pole would soon push the entire population of the Earth toward the equatorial zones; the civilized world would be thrown into utter chaos. Dunraven tried to warn the world of this impending doom. But no one cared to listen—not until it was too late. And soon the only question left unanswered was…could Mankind survive the coming of the Sixth Glacier?

CAST OF CHARACTERS

BENDER

Bender was a lucky reporter, often in the right place at the right time. His latest scoop…the imminent destruction of Earth!

STEPHEN REYNARD DUNRAVEN

His fascination with Paleontology led to the discovery of an impending ice age—but would the world heed his warnings?

CLARA DUNRAVEN

Junoesque—tall, shapely, and strong—she was her father's daughter and possessed an earnest desire to help the needy.

BERNARD ILMORE BULGER

He was the quintessential editor-in-chief, and sent his top man, Bender, to investigate Dunraven's predictions of doom.

PAUL EBERLE

He and the Dunravens were longtime friends, so it was easy to understand why he had his eye on the lovely Clara.

MAJOR REGINAL CUMMINS

Ever the military man, he thrived in adversity, and bumbled with the social graces, but a good man to have around in a tough spot.

THE SPIDERS

What about the spiders…? The only thing Dunraven knew about them was their obvious inability to survive.

THE SIXTH GLACIER

By
MARIUS

ARMCHAIR FICTION
PO Box 4369, Medford, Oregon 97504

*For more information about Armchair Books and products, visit our
website at…*

www.armchairfiction.com

Or email us at…

armchairfiction@yahoo.com

CHAPTER ONE
I Interview a Man with a Hobby

THE *Scientific News*, was a semi-technical monthly which catered to the scientifically minded laymen as much as it did to the scientists to whom mechanics, chemistry, or astronomy meant bread and board. Old Hillsboro had founded the paper nearly a quarter of a century ago when scientific periodicals were rarer than they are now and laymen, who had a predilection for the perusal of such a periodical, were rarer yet. His youngest son, the family's pride, had been my roommate at Princeton during our student days, and the friendship that later developed between his father and me, put me on the staff of the *Scientific News*.

Bulger, Bernard Ilmore Bulger was his whole name, was the editor-in-chief. A dried-up and garrulous little old man with an abnormally large head, a veteran of the editorial desk and one to whom the very air that he breathed meant no more than did the black and white pages of the *Scientific News*. To the little that he ever deigned to write, for he delved in science but feebly, he signed himself as BIB. Yesterday I stood face to face with him in the untidy, paper-littered inner recess of his sanctum. He glanced up at me from beneath his green eyeshade, as he slowly chewed the wet stub of an unlit cigar, his blue Nordic eyes twinkling merrily behind the powerful glasses of his spectacles.

"You here at last, eh?" he said rather a bit curtly, I thought. His voice was dry and raspy, the words snapping out of his mouth in a staccato-fashion, like the bullets out of a machine-gun. Then, without allowing me time for a reply, he continued, "Care to see Dunraven, eh? You know Dunraven?"

"I—which—who—Dunraven?" I began a bit uncertain and hesitating.

"Oh, come, come," snapped the little man, a bit irritated. "Dunraven the old street-car magnate. Stephen Reynard Dunraven who lives in the big white house on West Eighty-Third Street. You know the place well, or at least you ought to know it, you've been chasing up and down there ever since last Christmas. Take a run up there now, eh?" He stopped short.

"WHAT am I to see this Mr. Dunraven, street-car magnate, about?" I asked, taking advantage of the pause in his Niagara of words.

"About a hobby which he's got."

"A hobby. I see."

"Yes, he's nuts over some kind of a science study—Polontogy, or something. I know very little of such stuff. Out of my line entirely. I'm electricity, you know, pure and simple. Was raised on it. Suckled on the love of volts and amperes with my mother's milk. Pa was one of Bell's first disciples and I drink current out of a storage battery, so to speak."

"Paleontology, the science of the long ago," I interrupted him. "I see. So I am to interview him on paleontology. But what is this hobby of his that you speak of?"

"That's it. Paleontology, as you call it. That's his hobby. That and keeping mum. Heavens, but that man, when he wants to get way back into his shell; has all the qualities of an oyster. But you run along now and interview him. You know a thing or two about this paleontology. At least young Hillsboro used to take it quite to heart at college—bones and fossils and such things, and you roomed with him. Something of it ought to have stuck to you. So run along now and try to get a write-up for the next issue. You had better hurry."

His desk chair tilted forward to its natural position with a squeak and his huge head fell down.

"One moment please. What's old Dunraven and his hobby been doing? Anything out of the way?

"Oh yes." The eyes twinkled and his walnut-face peered up at me once more, and again the big chair squeaked a protest as he leaned backwards. "He's been running about the country for a year or so now making lots of noise about a change in weather that is soon to come. A—"

"It is kind of warm for spring."

"Warm? No, no. Good heavens, man, no. Not warm. Cold. Cold is what he wants, and lots of it, and don't you forget that when you're on West Eighty-Third street. Much cold. A coming glacier that is even now on its way, ready to freeze up the world. A new ice age, the pre-historic glacial period of the post-Pliocene of a hundred thousand years ago all over again. Snow and ice to be as far south as Arizona. Sleigh riding on Palm Beach."

He gave vent to a hen-cackle of a laugh at this bit of witticism. His face became redder. Then once again a wrinkled countenance and a pair of boyish eyes were confronting me.

"You see, he's been out paleontology-izing somewhere in north Mexico where he ran across some old Indian ruins, Aztec or something—very old. Well, he got together a Greaser pick-and-shovel crew and started digging. Pretty soon they unearthed a city, a very ancient city, mostly dust. It proved to be the abode of a hitherto unheard of civilization that flourished in its prime, about the time when you and I were jumping about on the tree-tops and cracking each others' skulls whenever the fight was on. A nation lived there when the Neanderthal man ran wild all over Europe. To make a long story short, he claims that he found a moulded and time-defaced tablet of gold in the ruins of one of the ancient buildings, and after a crowd of Egyptologists and experts on hieroglyphic picture writing got through with it, up pops the old fellow with a warning of another ice age soon to come, just like the one the world had a thousand centuries ago. New York, London, Paris, Tokyo, all of them are to be crushed and buried underneath a mile of ice. Pretty good story, eh? He wrote to practically every scientific and pseudo-scientific paper in this country and in England. He wrote to many papers that are not scientific. These rich men with hobbies never stop at anything. And he became much peeved because no one paid any attention to him. Regular sore-head. Earle of the *Science-Union*, a weekly, was one of the few who took him up. He wrote Dunraven, asking for a brief statement of facts. Earle himself told me that Dunraven's reply required quires of paper to print. It was at least fifty-thousand words long. He condensed it into four columns of print and let his readers have it, together with the old man's picture, whereupon Dunraven wrote him again—a long letter—telling him just what kind of an editorial ass he was. Then he shut up shop altogether and refused to talk paleontology to anyone. He's still sore. Pretty vain, eh?"

"And I am to interview him about—"

"About this discovery of his, the coming ice age, the sixth one. We've had five already, and now, so says Dunraven, a new glacier is due. And who can tell but that the old bird may be right? But be careful. The old fellow, so I hear, is down with the gout and not very cheerful, and his temper was never of the best. But you're big enough to look out for yourself, though I hardly believe he would be violent. At least while he is suffering from the gout. You ought to be able to handle him all right. You've been running around with his daughter ever since her dress caught fire at that poor children's fund Christmas tree party last year, when you played hero. Well, none of the other boys are any too anxious. At any rate get a line on it by hook or crook. May be more to it than we suspect and it pays to be first. Anything is legitimate in this game, you know. We're the ones responsible. Now git."

STEPHEN REYNARD DUNRAVEN, practically sole owner of the Seaboard Rapid Transit, had never played true to the rich man hero of fiction. He had not come over in the steerage, a poor immigrant boy, had never been a bare-footed country lad, nor a ragged city street Arab nor had he worked himself to riches and fame by his own efforts and ability. On the contrary, he was the pampered only son of wealthy Sir Cecil Dunraven, an English nobleman, who came, saw, and conquered on this side of the Atlantic. His youth, just as his early manhood, was spent with the complete abandon of those to whom time and expense are nothing. When his father, the old British peer, died, he left all of his worldly goods to his only heir and so, though nominally only, Stephen Reynard became the guiding hand of an entire traction trust. In reality, however, the gaylights claimed him as their own, and though later years had tended to sober him down, he still retained much of the colorful attire and the love of the adventurous, that marks the gay-blade. Then, when an unrelenting nature began to insist upon tolls long overdue and gout and asthma laid heavy hands upon him, he ceased to offer further worship at the gay altar of Bacchus and the energy which once upon a time had been expanded on Broadway, in Deauville, and at Monte Carlo was now given vent more sedately in the realms of science. In the clay with which he was moulded had been mixed a quantity of that stuff which the world knows as stick-to-it-iveness. He had the virtue, the blind virtue, of perseverance, the bulldog's grit for hanging on. Just as pleasures had claimed him in his youth with a force which an outraged nature alone was able to tear asunder, so in later and more sober years, that which took the place of the gay, white lights held this never quiet man. Paleontology became such a hobby to him as photography is to the inveterate Kodak fiend or stamp collecting to the incurable, rabid chaser after old postage stamps. And just as at one time he lived his life in an atmosphere filled with wine, music, and laughter, so now he dwelled in a primordial atmosphere of musty catacombs, dusty ruins, and ancient cities, the inhabitants of which had long ago become one with the elements from which they had sprung, a fanatical worshipper at the altar of dry mummies, resurrected dinosaurs, and Piltdown skull alike.

An immaculate and time-ravaged butler, a heritage of the Dunraven estate, ushered me into the presence of the prematurely aged traction magnate. He was in his study— sunk deep in the soft depths of a plush chair, one of his feet propped up on a stack of velvet cushions and a basketful of tiny, fragile bits of bones spread over on his lap.

'Lo, Bender," he grumbled, when he caught sight of me, then more softly, "Clara will be back soon. Come here and sit down next to me." His tone implied that he was not in the best of moods.

"Been having a messy lot of trouble lately with some of these periodicals that call themselves scientific," he opened the conversation abruptly, as was his habit.

"I see." I was preparing for an opening and had to be careful.

"Of course you've heard of my little 'find' in Mexico. An ancient ruin, very ancient, a city a thousand centuries old. A city that was old when man was still in the tree-tops and the caves. The dailies and a few of your scientific sheets gave it a write-up, but very little, indeed. Yet, Bender, the future of all civilization hangs on it—as if by a thread. I'm not exaggerating a bit. All civilized life."

He paused meditatively enthralled in his bones. I broke into the silence.

"That is the very reason why I am here, Mr. Dunraven," I began in almost apologetic tone. "I am, as you know, connected with a periodical that—"

I stopped short, for he had started to snort like an angry bison.

"Uh-huh. Oh, yes. The *Scientific News,* a sheet that caters to those who want their science cut and dried, and made up in pill form, energyless ones who lack the spine to fight or the brain to reason out a thing for themselves. Make-believe Pasteurs, milksop Galileos, parrot Marconis. So they've given me a tumble at last, eh. Even send their hound pups on my trail. Getting scared, or what? Too cold already? The ice is on its way, eh? Or maybe the prospects of a golden harvest to be reaped on the scientific back of old Steve Dunraven? No? Then can it really be that the glacier story has finally penetrated even a sub-mediocre cranium and that this is the first yelp for help out of the scared pups? Out with it, young fellow. What's stirring in the editorial circle?"

His manner, though brusque, had the tone of the curious man behind it, and I felt somewhat reassured. Emboldened I opened my mouth as if to speak but he stopped me with a gesture. He was vain and to him, this was the sweet nectar of revenge. I allowed him to proceed uninterrupted and was a silent listener to a half hour of declamations directed at the heads of a score of editors.

"Your own paper, the *Scientific News,*" he wound up his tirade, glaring at me, "is the best of this sordid lot, but even so it falls short of the mark. Nets the tiny fish but lets the big ones go—the important ones which really count."

He had lost all of his former heat and fury which I feared would develop into apoplexy, and was now more of the lecturer or the teacher before the class. He rang a bell and almost instantly a noiseless Jap serving-man appeared, entering on feline feet. He took a brief order for refreshments with dark, immobile features, and then retired as silently as he had come.

"Ido," remarked the stout amateur of science, "an Oriental relic as silent and as expressionless as any Budelha statuette of his native East. Strange people these Orientals—at least, strange to us."

The Jap serving-man came and went again, cat-like, silent.

"Now," said the scientist, settling back on his soft seat and raising his glass, "I will tell you a story."

CHAPTER TWO
The Man with a Hobby Tells a Story

ABOUT a year ago and despite my gout, which is bothering me now," continued the talker amid the clinking of chipped ice against fragile glass, "I decided to ramble to and fro in the sandy wastelands of Mexico in pursuit of my hobby. Mexico, abounding in remains historic, pre-historic, savage, semi-savage, and primordial, is a veritable Paradise for the archeologist and the paleontologist, as well as for the seeker after historical facts. It is a fertile and still only slightly explored field for every science, from Zoology to Sociology. It had civilizations when Rome was young. Square mile after square mile even today lies unexplored between our border and that of Central America and no discovery above or beneath that soil would surprise me one whit."

"Near a little railroad town on the Sur Pacifico del Mejico, named Hermosillo, Dame Fortune so twisted the webs of my life that I had the luck to run into a young mining engineer who had just returned from an unfortunate gold-seeking venture along the Yaqui River. He had barely escaped with his life from that almost forbidden territory of America's most savage of redmen. His partner, an aged metallurgist and a man of scientific inclinations, had been killed by the Yaquis and among his scanty belongings, the youthful engineer and gold-hunter had found a crude map hastily drawn with pencil on a brown paper bag. Time and rough usage had acted to obliterate the map and as the young man was not possessed of much patience, the deciphering was a failure and so on the following day the unfortunate gold-hunter started back for his native England.

"By all means this should have been the natural end of my story, yet the twists of chance were such that the disappointed Englishman left his map behind him and on the following night, not having anything more useful at hand, curiosity, that virtue of virtues of the scientific mind, tempted me to ponder over the roughly sketched map on the Manila paper bag.

"It showed roughly the sketch of a hill or mound. A hillock such as are common among high mountains, was set at one end of it like a tiny nodule on a very round potato. A poorly sketched cabin with the almost obliterated words 'house' and 'ancient ruins' was indicated at the foot of this nodule. The rest of it was measurements and names, out of which I could make nothing. Upon a close scrutiny I managed to decipher the all but obliterated word 'Magdalena' and an indicating arrow at the extreme right of the map. It was the key to the puzzle.

"OF course it is needless for me to tell you that I allowed very little time to pass ere I was at the scene so obscurely depicted on the map. A bloodhound of science must follow even the remotest of clues, and so one day later the little town of Magdalena became my home and headquarters. On the morning of the second day I went forth to investigate. The third day found me wild with excitement.

"The mound was there. The map had not lied nor was it the idle offspring of some over-imaginative mind in search of something to do, and my chase had not been empty. At one end of it, as indicated, was the mound and at the foot of this stood a ramshackle apology for a cabin. Years ago, probably, some gypsy peon had stopped long enough in his vagabondage to raise a crop of corn or beans there and had built this little abode for the shelter of himself and his family. Beside it appeared what at one time undoubtedly had been the entrance to a shaft or excavation. Upon examination this proved to be about ten or twelve feet deep and about five feet wide, and had all the appearances of a very old well which had gone unused for many years. I decided to investigate.

"With the help of a hired peon, I started to dig and we dug laboriously to a depth of about twenty feet into the soft bowels of the earth and then the bottom caved in beneath us, and we fell an extra ten feet. My half-breed helper was badly scared but this newest discovery only augmented my ardor. I decided to go deeper yet and, despite the pleas and warnings of Pancho, recommenced digging. I was rewarded amply, for after a very few strokes of my pick I struck rock, or rather brick. I cleared away some loose earth and you can imagine my surprise when I picked up the fragment of a time-hallowed wall. A minute later, with throbbing heart, I was contemplating a part of some very ancient structure made up of bricks of a dull red hue. I shouted a 'Eureka' which almost scared the wits out of Pancho who, armed with a shovel, retreated to one end of the gloomy pit as if expecting an immediate attack from a madman.

"The short twilight was now in the skies overhead, and so deciding to follow up this bizarre clue on the morrow, I made use of dangling rope, and together with Pancho, emerged to safety and mediocrity.

"The next day I returned to Magdalena for additional assistance.

"The tale that the post-Pliocene strata into which I had dug unfolded to me was one which no man had ever been told before. The record, ever so ancient, that Time as it passed had left behind it beneath the mound, to let the world know of its slow but sure predatory raids, was set before me awaiting only the translation which the geologist and the archeologist alone can give. The entire story of the re-elevation of the continents and the restoration of milder climates that so marked the post-glacial years and brought on the advent of true man, was open before my eyes in this little excavation.

"WELL, I'll not go into any details of the excavation work itself. Suffice it to say that it was within the comparatively short period of three months that our picks, shovels, and bars had cleared away enough of Nature's ancient deposits to reveal to daylight a new long lost city, or rather a long lost civilization, a civilization which soon proved itself to have been hoary with years, at the period when the flat-skulled ape man was Nature's highest bid toward humanity. Now fat lizards warmed themselves on the hot sands that covered it. Further clearing revealed ruins of walls and caved-in cellars where the dust heaps of Time reigned supreme. Here and there remained a part of a tower or fragile wall, still erect, which gave mute testimony of bygone days of pomp and grandeur, and over it all, like some Time-ravaged sentinel, a tall, broad-based edifice, almost intact, raised its head. It was the brick balustrade on the top of this that my inquisitive pick had struck. Starting out as a pyramid and almost solid the tall tower went up heavenward to about one-fifth of its intended height only to become a slender, flat-roofed octagon-shaped steeple, which resembled a very tall lighthouse set on a pyramid rock, or a gigantic church tower overlooking the plains. The pyramid part of it was of solid masonry, roughly hewed stones placed one on top of the other in the manner of the tombs of old Egypt's kings. Its sole interior was a single passageway full of debris, about two feet wide and about five feet high. The tower was of small rust-colored bricks, and reinforced with crude iron girders as are the towers of the modern skyscraper.

"It was to this mammoth tower and all of its indications toward scientific remunerations, that I henceforth gave all of my time and attention. With the aid of two savants, whom I had hurriedly summoned to the spot, and an extra-large crew of intrinsically indolent peon day-laborers, we had cleared away, in two weeks, practically all of the debris that for so long a time had remained untouched. As dust, stone, and earth reluctantly left their ancient homes there was revealed to our astonished eyes the unmistakable outlined likenesses of galleries, laboratories, and classrooms. Even Time, through its slow and silent raids of countless years, was unable to obliterate entirely the traces and outlines that shelves, test-tubes, and books had left behind them as ghosts of a bygone glory. Even the unpracticed eye of the layman was able to see as much. Brown rags that seemed to melt beneath the touch told mute tales of age-old volumes, tiny bits of vitreous matter of glass tubes and jars, and moulded metal told of bench and shelf.

"And now comes the pinnacle of my tale. Without it, in fact, there would have been no tale at all. Searching for further scientific data, I found the gold-plated tablet which warned of the glacier—the sixth glaciation period of the last ice age, which is on us even today. It was set in stone, cracked, moulded stone,—roughhewn granite. It was encrusted with such accumulation as a thousand centuries alone can give and required three whole days of slow and careful washing a scraping to bring forth to light the hieroglyphics that told of the ice to come—the impending sixth glacier.

"HOW the world greeted my warning you know very well. Where it was not indifference, it ridiculed with base, cheap ridicule, in which I suspect that envy took no small part. Men were too busy chasing pennies, lying, stealing, killing, for them to pay any heed to a scientist, who shouted silly tales, of the north-pole coming down and crushing their fifty centuries of gatherings and accumulations beneath a mile thickness of ice and snow. I gave voice to my warnings of danger through that moulder of public opinion—the daily press, and through periodicals which claimed science as their fetish. Because I was 'old man' Steve Dunraven, ex-street-car magnate, political power, one time Broadway cut-up, and a very rich man with a queer scientific eccentricity, up popped the editorial ears for a while. Every daily had a column or two and every magazine printed my picture. But it was too much to ask for more. Lost in a maze of scandals politics and other juicy tit-bits of lasciviousness, an occasional word or two did appear in one sheet or the other, but not for very long, you may be sure. True, a scientifically inclined editor or two did take up my story, but, somehow or other, it seemed too harsh, too dreadful to ponder long upon. People hate to know of dangerous things, even when they are near. Someone invented a new type of non-refillable soda-water bottle and the spaces which should have belonged to the Sixth Glacier were given over to mediocrity and soda water bottles, and a mediocre-minded reading public had gotten its demands. But what's the difference? They'll know soon enough that it's here when it arrives.

"Would you care to see the plate I found?"

I did care. In fact, I was eager to see it. A young and ambitious writer on the staff of an esteemed scientific publication, I hungered after something like this, a chance to show the stuff of which each and every one of us thinks that he or she is made of. Like a carnivore mad with appetite, I pounced upon this juicy meat handed out by Chance. What an opportunity! What a blow at those supercilious ones above me, my senior wise-acres. A multi-millionaire and trust-head, a by no means unworthy amateur of science, and a possible world-savior taking me, poor little me, into his confidences.

CHAPTER THREE
Out of the Long Ago

BEARING with it the musty aura of an epoch of bygone eons, the plate, in size like the top of the average kitchen table, seemed to tell mute stories of civilizations now dim and distant in the oblivion of the past, of peoples now long ago dead, whose histories were in the mould when man was young. Time had dealt roughly with it as it does with all else. It had fringed its metal edges and through countless centuries had torn gaps in its surface. Yet Time plays freakish pranks and so much of the hieroglyphics were legible, that even I, an entire ignoramus as far as Egyptology was concerned, was able to discern that this plate would never be out of place among the many stone and metal echoes from the past which Egypt, and the entire Levant have given forth from cave, excavation and ruin. We grace our museums with them at the same time they allow the scientist to look behind the mistiest curtains of the past.

"Well," grumbled my host, assuming an indifferent, almost hostile air, which was belied by the satisfied look on his face.

"It's great, wonderful," I answered, and a moment later the door of the big room was swept open on almost noiseless hinges and Clara entered silently and nimbly, like a kitten. She broke a very awkward silence.

Clara was tall, of the Juno type, a bit too tall for a woman, I often thought. Yet such types did the sculptors of old love to let live on in marble form. She carried her weight gracefully, like a gigantic ocean-greyhound or a tall grenadier. Her features, a bit small, told of northland forebears, while her sky-blue eyes sang merry sagas of Arctic seas, on which rode the storms of the boreal lords. Then too, if one looked close enough; one could observe, behind that petulant, girlish mask, a bit of the bulldog and of the tiger that was her father. Clara was a Dunraven, no mistake about that.

During the meal that followed the girl's arrival, the rich amateur of science was still very voluble concerning his Mexican discovery. He told of the various scientific definitions of the causes of the five previous glacial periods; and the theory of polar earthquakes, great and fierce enough to elevate the northernmost and southernmost regions of this globe and send millions upon millions of tons of Arctic ice on a wicked errand to the temperate zones, was described by him. He told of the theory which has it that approximately once every twenty-one thousand years the coincidence of a northern hemispheric winter through the precession of the equinoxes, with an Aphelion of the earth and thus the greater distance and the longer wintry absence of our solar life-giver causing a longer, more rigid, and more rigorous winter, which of course was that much Greek to me—of the theory of interfering atmospheric agencies and a consequent shifting of the sea's cold water currents, and he finished with a theory or two of his own, to all of which I gave a politely attentive ear.

"But," he continued, laying down his napkin with a thud, "we were all wrong, every mother's son of us, scientists and all, and every theory is but so much nonsense. No earthquake, since this bit of an ore started to solidify, could be big enough, no winter harsh enough, and no shifting of a score of Gulf Streams effective enough to cause a world of ice and snow to leave its polar home and come down as glaciers toward the warmer climes. Bigger agencies must prevail—outside agencies. How about a frigid space in this endless cosmos, for instance? Imagine a huge frigid belt in interstellar space, this unbounded vastness that holds all, and through which frigid area our tenth rate sun with its escort of tiny balls must pass periodically, to freeze our water to solid ice, as we rush hither and thither through eternity and orbit space.

"THE plate," he resumed after a huge draught of hot coffee, "was a puzzler from the start. The half-baked Egyptologists and hieroglyphic experts at my service could do but little with it, though credit is due them that they tried. Of course, some concessions must be made to the fact that it is not such a one as the average hieroglyphic expert is at all likely to encounter. Although it told its ancient story in direct form, just as those ancient historians of Babylon and Chaldea recorded their battles, sieges, hunts, and feasts on the stones, which once upon a time graced their palaces and now fill our museums, this story was such a one that no expert who had expended a lifetime in delving into the lives of Pharaohs or the wars of the ancient Cretans could be expected to comprehend it. Accustomed as they were to picture-writings, which depicted historical events, religious ceremonies, deaths, and such, what chance could they possibly have had with the representation of a ball or sphere surrounded entirely by a hazy, cloud-like aura, and covered all over with cone-shaped upheavals? Then there is also a series of very puzzling "chicken scratches" or markings on it. The experts had already given it up as a bad job, but it was just where they left off, baffled, that I began. Armed as I was with my knowledge of paleontology, which as you know is like a hobby to me, I could break my way into the puzzling strongholds of the crypt which their wisdom in the reading of historical pictures never allowed them to enter. I knew well that the tablet had to do with events that took place in its hey-day of a thousand centuries ago. The Egyptologist does not delve into the past for one-tenth of that time. He draws his conclusions from what, to the delver into the primordial, would seem but the modern world. The picture of an ice-covered world in the throes of a gigantic frigid epoch spent in frigid space, could not be solved by men, who could see no farther back into our past than ten centuries, the tail end of the Neolithic Time where the paleontologist generally leaves off. To them it was a mystery. A few even put it down to a primitive practical joke. I alone saw its worth and later its terrible meaning. Luckily the warning had come in time.

"One night as I pondered over the tablet which I had obtained out of the long ago, the thought of its great age came suddenly into my mind and would not allow itself to be dislodged. It was over a hundred thousand years ago, the day of the flat-skulled Neanderthal man and the jaw-bone war-club, that it first saw light. I mused on this tusked and hirsute forebear of ours, who because of a nobler brain lived to propagate its race while the stronger ones died. Too slow to catch the contemporary animals smaller than himself, too weak to give combat to the bigger ones, he in his hyena-like existence was more often the hunted than the hunter. They were hard, tough days, those early days when our race was still in the crucible. Today your neighbor was your friend, tomorrow he might be a hungry enemy. And then, I mused to myself, came the ice, the fifth glacier of the last ice age. In an instant I was out of my reverie. The key to the puzzle had been found. The ball was our own globe, this tenth rate handful of dirt which we call our own. Fool that I had been not to notice that before, with its seven sister planets around it, its tiny satellite nearby, and the rays of the sun cutting into one corner of the picture and only to disperse and lose themselves, as though they were powerless, in the icy cloud which surrounded the rotund earth. One of my experts had even remarked it as being an astronomical or even an astrological study, but of no importance to science. The jagged protuberances were hills of ice, highly magnified so as to give them their worldly import, that left only the most torrid part of our globe out of the realms of the glaciers. There the hot sun of the equator proved a barrier to the cyclopean fields of ice which vise-like held the central strip of the earth in their chilly jaws. The cloudy aura around the globe could show only one thing—that we had run into a vast frigid nebula in space as our tiny solar caravel floated on this endless ocean of eternity. Another glaciation was close at hand and perhaps was even now upon us.

"NOW, as you have probably noticed already on the plate are five sets of horizontal crisscross figures, one beneath the other, just like so many "hen scratches" in barnyard sand, and in indicating arrow points from each one of these to the frozen globe. At first they puzzled me greatly. Six vertical lines, each one of them about four inches long and as straight as any arrow. Across the first five is drawn a number of horizontally placed cross lines one on the first, two on the second, three on the third, eight on the fourth, and five on the fifth. The last one is bereft of any crossings. After hours of pondering, during which time I became a grizzly bear to my household, I came upon the happy solution that this was the numerical system of those people who passed away centuries before we came and left behind them the warning of the ice. Each crossed vertical bar was to them what a numerical figure is to us. A blank bar meant zero, one cross a one, two crosses a two, and so on, each numerical unit in its proper place, units, tens, hundreds, thousands. The five numbers on the plate, one below the other, were the same, one, two, three, eight, five, zero, one-hundred and twenty-three thousand, eight-hundred and fifty. A long number of years; a long, long time. To pass through so vast a history, the space of the five periods of glaciation of the fifth ice age, each one separated by more than a thousand centuries, almost one million years in all, their civilization must indeed have been a hoary one. Five glacial inroads with their relentless icy fury, came and went through the ages of their history, each one left destruction in its wake, and yet these people still lived on, lived on long enough to warn us of the sixth. Came the troglodyte, tusked and hairy, only to disappear in the darkness of the past, leaving behind him his handle-less flints to show that he had been a being in this grand scheme of things. Yet these people continued to carry on their civilization. Where, or who their remnants are, who can say?"

He stopped abruptly and glared at me. I thought it high time for me to give voice to something. Fortunately a question occurred.

"How," I asked, "did you deduce that the necessary one hundred and twenty-three thousand odd years are gone by and the time for the sixth glacier is here?"

"Geology, my dear young fellow, told me as plainly as a calendar could have done, the approximate age of the buried ruins. The post-Pliocene strata had covered them entirely. That they were pre-historic, paleontologic, I was certain beyond a doubt. Skeletal remains, flat-headed, thick-boned, tusked skulls, long bones of ape-like arms and short, crooked legs, gave me so much mute testimony and corroborated my guesswork. I was viewing the remnants of a city which at the most conservative of estimates was well over a thousand centuries old. What business the ape man had there I am still at a loss to understand. The brains that were able to erect so grand a city were by no means enclosed in flat, thick-boned skulls. A nobler race, surely, once upon a time had lived, wrought, and died there. Geologically I was able to discern that this spectre of a city was of the early part of the post-Pliocene, in round numbers about a hundred thousand years ago. This much was certain for the story of the strata is a faultless diagram of the earth's early history. And that was the time of the last glacial era.

"Of course, it might not have been due for ·ten thousand years yet to come; but then again, I thought, it might be on its way even now, silently hurrying southward to destroy us. I did not care to disturb a satisfied world from its complacency with the tale of a probable ice age, perhaps ten thousand years hence. Such far off things would not interest most of us. Oh, if I could only be certain enough to bring it close to home.

"ONE day nearly half a year after I had first sunk pick into the sandy soil of Mexico and unearthed this warning, I happened to be talking with Professor Roane, the old man on Mt. Hamilton who has spent most of his lifetime at the eyepiece of a huge telescope. He has a few brochures and an astronomical treatise or two to his credit, and is an unquestioned authority on anything in the skies. During our conversation, he happened to remark in the most off-hand way possible, that a hazy nebula, almost invisible, had suddenly popped up in the direction of Orion. It appeared as if a very light mist had floated in front of his telescope, and like an ethereal pall it hung suspended in space about a billion miles away. As days went by it became larger and drew nearer. Next it was found that it was not traveling at all; that on the contrary, it was fixed and rigid in space. Instead, our entire solar system, was moving toward it at many million miles a day on our grand journey through orbit space. 'Eureka,' I cried, for at last I had found my frigid belt in space, the cloud of coldness of the golden plate, the cloud that was to bring the ice and usher in a reign of Death. The hundred and twenty-three thousand eight-hundred and fifty years were up, and the northern ice was free again and even now was on its way. The warning had not been found too late. There was still time for action.

"Well, for a time I foolishly nursed the asinine notion that a grateful world would be polite enough to give me at least a bit of attention. But, bah! Look at them now!"

I LEFT a half hour later. A newer world had opened up before me and in the dimness of it I saw the stout amateur paleontologist and multi-millionaire traction man and his pretty daughter. I gazed for a while at the sky. It was inky black, for the moon had not yet arisen, but the ebon monotony was broken in a hundred million places by so many tiny pin-pricks which scintillated like fairy magic lanterns in the void above me. No sign, no trace of the ice cloud of the warning plate from the hoary past. Even the air of the night was too warm for springtime, yet I shivered instinctively for I knew only too well that the man had not talked without cause.

CHAPTER FOUR
The First Warning Cry

ONE day the news from Copenhagen came by the International News service, that the Arctic exploring auxiliary ship *Sven Hedin*, had sent a wireless to her home port, Copenhagen, the Danish capital, telling of immense ice floes in the vicinity of 83° N.L. Twenty-four hours later her commander, Captain Martin Jensen, wirelessed his home office that the *Sven Hedin*, had been entirely locked in by a sudden freeze and an inexplicable rush of ice floes from the north. He commented on the strangeness of such a situation at that season of the year, and reported that as far as he was able to observe, a rugged, peaked ice field was the supreme monarch. An hour later he sent out his danger call which at the same time was his farewell. A terrific boreal snow-storm was even then in progress and rigorous Arctic winter was being ushered in in June. This was the last ever heard of Captain Jensen or the *Sven Hedin*.

It was only then that I realized at last that the glacier had really come. I looked out of my window and down on the street below. People were walking by unconcernedly; none of them seemed to be in a hurry. Some little children were playing a game, on the sidewalk, two larger boys were catching ball in the center of the street, while a small group of bobbed haired school girls were coming merrily from school. No one appeared to heed the warning of the ice, yet the crack of doom was even now upon them. Could it, after all, really be so? I questioned myself; and then I thought of the little news item from Denmark and saw a mental picture of the ill-starred exploring ship crushed in the icy embraces of the boreal deluge, far off in the north. For a moment Nature's first law, that of self-preservation, gained the upper hand, and I had a vague notion of a tropical flight. Clara played a big part in it. A fleeting cinema display of a bamboo bungalow on some sandy shore beneath the blazing sun of the equator, and Stephen Dunraven's pretty daughter near-by, passed before my mental eyes, lingering but for a second. It was instantly followed by that of a northern world locked in the cruel throes of snow and ice, ragged, cold mountains that seemed to press against the leaden sky, covering in its depths, that which at one time had been a civilization, and I shuddered involuntarily. With Clara (for some reason or other I could never get her out of my mental pictures) I was living in a snow igloo, hunting walrus and eating blubber. I wore a furry Eskimo tamiak and walked on wide unwieldy snow-shoes, racket-like frames filled with reindeer sinews. The telephone bell rang sharply, a very prosaic everyday occurrence, far from dreams and reveries.

Stephen Dunraven was at the other end of the wire and his gruff voice invited me to come over immediately: He had something very important to tell me. He was witty a bit—

something about a trip to Panama and having reserved seats on the boat before the rush. An hour later I was on West Eighty-Third Street.

"I am in touch with the 'Land's End' of the world," he let me know even before I had entered the door of his den, "and have just received word from Spitsbergen, far away off northernmost Russia. A wireless to Leningrad has it that a huge drop in temperature has pervaded the entire northern part of the country and goes on to tell of immense ice floes in the seas around Spitsbergen and Franz-Josef Land. This was three days ago. No more news has come from there since. But things have progressed there rapidly. That land was the first one to go and is even now under a hundred feet of ice. The glacier is on its way."

He paused and drew himself erect, a silent way of saying, "I told you so."

HUDSON BAY was heard from next, as it too entered the cold fringes of the frigid belt, and in two days it was silent. I awaited the glacier with a feeling that was not unmixed with bodily fear. At last we had entered the area of the cold spot in space which had thinned out into invisibility when we approached it.

The *Scientific News* was the first to warn the world, and combined its cry of danger with an apology and appreciation for the man whose early warning went unheeded. And the cries of distress from beyond the Arctic Circle did not go unheeded. The presses of the entire world soon took it up and a deluge of reporters soon flooded the big house on West Eighty-Third Street.

Then one day the temperature of New York City took a sudden drop of eighteen degrees. One noon it was seventy-two, the next noon it was fifty-four. The metropolitan cities of all the world sent in similar messages telling of similar woes. The coming cold was beginning to show its cruel teeth.

It was at this time that the rich amateur of science became irritated. The belated halo did not seem to fit him when revenge was so much sweeter. Almost overnight his home had become the much sought after Mecca of scared men and women and of enterprising reporters. To those few of the frightened ones to whom he deigned to give audience, his sarcastic advice was to buy land in Yucatan. "What to do here? Wish he knew. Why worry, what have *you* to lose? How much? Huh, what about myself with a street car line at stake? Oh, you'll build yourself another house farther south. Lots of vacant land in Brazil and the Argentine. How should *he* know where the frigid zone came from? Well, it can't be helped. It's not my fault, so please don't look at me like that. Nonsense, there was still ample time. The glacier will not be here tomorrow. No he couldn't say just how long it would stay or what it would do. He was no prophet. Well, then stick it out if you feel that way. Certainly it would destroy New York City. Other cities too—plenty of them." And so on and so forth.

Then came the news from Alaska, which brought the glacier closer to home, Juneau was under a hundred feet of ice. A huge moving sheet that extended for many miles over land and sea had suddenly popped up overnight and crushed the town, leaving no survivors to tell the tale. Alaska shipping, southward bound, was overcrowded and from the half dozen large seaports on the Pacific, three-score steamers were heading swiftly toward the land beyond the Bering Sea. A hundred thousand terrified refuges were even now moving southward overland or awaiting succor by the sea, killing, fighting, mobbing for life. Also much of the population of Canada and of the northernmost United States was already moving south. The southern cities were expecting a huge influx from the north and were preparing for it. So too were Mexico and the rest of the Latin-American countries, all of them getting in readiness for a vast and undisciplined army of terrified and desperate fugitives from the north.

In Europe and in Asia the situation was no different. From London to Moscow and Tokyo every city reported tremendous climatic changes and Stockholm had a snowstorm in July. Berlin told of huge ice cakes in the River Spree and the harbor of Leningrad was entirely frozen, locking in its icy embraces scores of ships of all nationalities. There had been severe riotings in both Copenhagen and Amsterdam, in which troops let loose machine-guns upon desperate mobs of citizens, Tokyo reported a drop of twenty degrees and Peking of twenty-six. The harbor of Vladivostok in Siberia had long ago become ice-bound and a series of huge blizzards had stopped all traffic on the trans-Siberian Railroad.

All this happened only one week after the first call of distress from Captain Jensen and his luckless ship, a prisoner in the Arctic Circle. The Sixth Glacier was knocking on mankind's door.

LIKE all of the northern and the far southern world, the population of the British Isles, Scandinavia, north Russia, the Teutonic countries, Japan, Siberia, and northern China were fleeing towards the equator before the icy menace from the pole. Towns became evacuated overnight; cities were deserted in a week's time. In London rioting and looting were rampant and armored cars, artillery, and tear-bombs were freely used by both the police and military. Spain and Italy had suddenly enacted very drastic immigration laws and a newest war-cloud was once more hanging ominously low over Europe. Every English seaport town was over-crowded with mad and excited people, anxious to leave their little island trap. Shipping was accompanied by bedlam-like scenes and several huge holocausts broke out on the wharves. Chinese soldiers in Peking and in other Chinese cities were killing panic-stricken Chinamen, who were mobbing government offices demanding free transportation to the south. Turkey very wisely opened up her doors to all newcomers and then went south herself. Budapest's slum districts were afire. There were revolutions in Romania, in Bulgaria, in Armenia, in Poland, and the Don Cossacks were demanding something or other. A queer race, this race of ours. News from overseas told of a heterogeneous jumble of terrific accounts of fires, murders, mobs, pillagings, riots, revolts, and mad attempts to flee the icy fury from the pole.

The day before the burning of London, and the subsequent fighting between armed mobs and the soldiers, found me once again a guest in West Eighty-Third Street. Edinburg had just told of a blizzard and Liverpool reported that the Mersey was almost solid and shipping circles were at their wit's end.

Due to their locations so much farther to the north than the cities of the western hemisphere, the countries of northern Europe and Asia suffered the advent of the glacier a good while before we did. India's torrid land is on one latitude with the central part of the United States, while Labrador and London are almost face to face. The Gulf Stream going north with its hotter waters from the equatorial regions, brings with it the heat that makes a temperate land out of the British Isles and the countries of northern Europe and then as this stream turns south again and becomes the cold Arctic Current, its frigid waters from the polar zones help to make the rigid winters of our otherwise warmer Atlantic seaboard.

A THRONG of people out of every walk in life had so surrounded the white mansion that a special cordon of police was found to be necessary. The amateur scientist, who had become internationally famous in one fortnight, had given strict orders to allow no one who had come without an invitation, into his home, and a big force of special detectives rigidly observed orders. A bullet-headed police-sergeant, wide of shoulders and huge of feet, accepted with a look of suspicion the story, that my invitation had been given over the telephone and thereby was of necessity, a verbal one. A minute later I was behind the huge door and in the presence of the amateur-scientific multi-millionaire. Three other men, one of them very stiff in an army officer's uniform, were also seated.

"How are you, Bender?" said the man of science in a somewhat gruff voice and without arising from his plush armchair. That over, he turned to the trio before me, as I slunk without noise into a rather unobtrusive part of the room and took the role of the silent though interested listener. The talker's voice implied a mixture of sarcasm and impatience. His mood seemed to verge on boredom.

"Of course..." (he was eying the khaki-clad man, a major-general in the army) "...the Antarctic regions will come north. That is they will expand because of the cold, as we enter the more frigid core of the nebula. It isn't cold yet. It hasn't really begun yet. We're only on the fringe of the belt. I cannot say exactly how far the glaciers will extend, though at a wanton guess I would put the latitudes of Buenos Aires and of, well let's say Los Angeles, as their respective border lines. Certainly not into the tropics. Those regions will be our sole refuge from the glacier and maybe our future homes, where our future years spent in the frigid belt, will be cool ones, while the northern and southern parts of our globe will be uninhabitable, maybe even unapproachable. I base my conclusions on the extent of the glaciers of the past, but don't let that keep you from moving to Brazil."

"Isn't this the end of the world?" broke in one of the civilians of the seated trio, a short, pudgy city official of advanced years and a very bald head. He appeared to be badly frightened.

"How should I know?" snapped out the hero of the times. "Am I a prophet?"

The little man reddened and said no more. The army officer glared at him.

"My advice, gentlemen," continued the erstwhile speaker, "would be a hurried southern flight for all of us. There is plenty of room in the tropics for everybody and the change will do lots of people good. Of course, those countries will not be as torrid as they are today. The frigid belt and the neighboring Arctic countries will see to that. The world has had its equatorial palm-gardens but their setting sun is even now at hand. The tropics will be temperate, with snowy winters and cool summers, lands of fir and pine. The temperate zones will be Arctic, and Lord knows what the Arctic zones will be. Yes, gentlemen, our winter days are here."

"BUT what about the population, the people?" The military man was speaking.

"Well, what about them?"

"They'll freeze." In an anxious tone of voice.

"They can get out, couldn't they? I see no one chained."

"Yes, yes, but..." he paused. "...imagine the exodus. Here in New York for instance, a city of five million of every class on earth—millions of men, women, and children, babes in arms, in a mad stampede toward the south. Riots, disaster, looting, murdering. Think of it. Washington has already ordered every available regiment northward. What would our meager transportation facilities amount to in the face of so huge an emigration? And the lands through which they need pass! Think of them. Barren, sir, that's what they'll be.

People will fight for food. Tear one another to pieces. It means war to the hilt.

"Trampled children, tired women falling by the roadside, the aged, the crippled abandoned…" (here I noticed that the corpulent city official was nervously fingering his derby hat) "…to a cruel fate. The terror-stricken people will rise against their superiors, upon whom they had learned to rely." (The corpulent one gave a sudden twitch and dropped his derby). "The southern states will become overcrowded and the result shall be war, because the refugees will be desperate men and women."

"I guess they will be," the scientist interrupted him.

The general had just opened his mouth to continue his tirade, when the city official interrupted again.

"Can't you help, sir?" he began in a very weak voice. "Can you suggest something?"

"Move to Cuba." (In an offhand manner).

"But the people?"

"Let them move to Cuba, too."

"There'll be mobs," the soldier resumed, "terrible fighting: caused by hunger and fear, and they'll stop at nothing."

"Oh, they'll find a way out, general. Of course, many will die, but just as many will be saved. Everyone can't be lucky."

The third man of the trio surrounding the scientist had spoken, and though his back was turned toward me, I immediately recognized the voice to be that of young Paul Eberle, an old friend of the Dunraven family, whose father at one time had been the partner in business and pleasure with the extraction head. I felt ill at ease, for I knew only too well that Paul Eberle had left his Chicago home for but one reason, and that reason was Clara.

THE feline-footed Jap serving-man entered, as silent as a tomb, and without noticing the presence of any of us, and with an expression like a vacuum, handed his employer a telegram. Stephen Dunraven read it very rapidly.

"News from the Antarctic, gentlemen," he said in a thrilled voice and with a slight sideway glance at the tall man in khaki. "I've been right again. Listen to this, 'Huge ice fields have covered Wilkesland entirely, a mile thick. Wilkesland, by the way, is that part of the Antarctic which lies directly south of Australia. Falkland Island is a second South Pole. The temperature of Buenos Aires is 14 degrees Fahrenheit, and three inches of snow fell last night in Rosario, three hundred miles upriver. Also there is fear for the Schwentner Antarctic Expedition, and that fear is only too well founded. Karl Schwentner has made his last exploring trip, rest assured. You see, gentlemen, I am well connected with the outside world even if I do but seldom leave my little castle on West Eighty-Third."

An uncomfortable silence followed. Paul yawned audibly. Obviously he was very indifferent to the conversation. The general was humbled, but he remained stiff and soldierly. The little city official (I think he was an alderman) was still nervously toying with his derby. Stephen Dunraven glared into empty space.

The little Jap, a coffee-colored statuette from the Orient, had stood immobile behind the corpulent magnate's chair, ever since he had brought in the telegram with its cataclysmic news.

"Better get your overcoat ready, Ido," said his employer. "Cold days are ahead of us. Winter soon. A big hill of ice is coming and it's coming fast. Yea, cold days soon."

The little dark-skinned fellow spread his mouth into a long grimace and showed a row of lacteal white teeth.

"Plenty warm in Nagasaki," he answered in a low tone, never moving from where he stood. "I go Nagasaki when cold ice come here."

"Plenty cold in Nagasaki too, Ido," responded the former speaker. "Soon ice everywhere. Better go Panama."

The Jap grinned once more, bowed, and then passed noiselessly through the door, where the gloom of the long hallway took him from our view.

AN hour later I was alone with the rich man whose hobby was science. A wild, rash idea entered my mind and I found myself unable to dislodge it. Paul Eberle's presence had put it there. I cannot recollect what I said, how I said it, or how much there was to it, but totaled up it amounted to a plea for Clara's hand. I have a faint recollection that it was as eloquent and as pathetic as it was lengthy, yet somehow or other it never affected the older man.

"See her about that, Bender, not me," he answered my fifteen minute speech in the most off-hand of tones and without looking up. As I left the house, I decided to take his advice. Faint heart ne'er won fair lady and a proposal by proxy is no proposal at all.

CHAPTER FIVE
The Fury from the Pole

ICELAND had become as its name implied, a land of ice. Newfoundland and Leningrad voiced their final cries of distress at one time and three days later both Scotland and Sweden reported the first sight of the moving fields of ice, and Norway followed in a belated message, a day after them. The transatlantic routes had become a death-trap of floating icebergs, Brobdingnagian mounds of ice that glittered like immense jewels in the sunlight. Airplane bombs of thermite proved ineffective in the face of this newest menace.

The southward migration of the vast hordes of northern Europe had already attained a prodigious magnitude with the stricken nations carrying to safety their priceless treasures of art. Military guards on the Swiss-Italian frontier had fired upon a caravan of scared burghers from Germany and Holland, killing many. War seemed imminent. A small fleet of British steamers loaded down to capacity with their human freight, were refused port at Barcelona, whereupon British warships opened fire upon that luckless Spanish town; the results were several beached vessels and a huge conflagration. North and south China were at one another's throats and the Japs disregarded openly the warnings from Washington that any further attempts to land emigrants on the shores of Hawaii or the Philippines would be considered an overt act of war. Every nation wanted to fight for what it considered its rights, if only for a few days.

On this side of the Atlantic, the situation was very similar. On the day following the Scotch message, the state of Alabama, already plethoric with northern refugees and an unhappy victim of every manner of vandalism, decided to shut her doors. The militia was quickly mobilized and artillery and machine-guns were placed along all highways, railroads, and rivers. Sanguinary fighting took place between the guardsmen and the refugees. Other southern states soon followed suit and added fresh fuel to the already lively fracas.

NEW YORK CITY was in the grip of terror and uproar. Her East Side ghetto districts were a series of noisy madhouses day and night with which police and militia both were unable to cope. The inherent emotional trait of the peasant manifested itself in wild orgies, mad religious revivals which bordered on insanity, and desperate riots which always terminated in the shedding of blood of overworked policemen and of fire-brigades. The other districts, however, were more sober. Viewing it all in retrospect, it appears to me to have been just like an angry beehive that had been disturbed by rude hands; bees flying about everywhere, buzzing madly and bent on wicked errands, yet in a hodge-podge, aimless, and crazy way, combating one another in an effort to evade the foe of all. Nobody appeared to have any direction save a hazy tendency to the south, and no one had any idea how to go or what to do there. Wrecks of cars lined the roadsides unheeded by anybody, and here and there a gruesome funeral pyre of shattered wood and twisted steel told its mute story of what scared men can do. Railroad service was irregular and congested to an overflow. Wrecks were innumerable and the death list was a long one. The sixth Glacier was indeed beginning to take its toll of lives long before it came upon the scene.

ON the eleventh day of July, England reported a very severe blizzard, which was accompanied by a prodigious drop in the thermometer. The same report told also how northern Scotland had finally been reached by the advancing fields of ice. Christiana now Oslo, Norway's capital city, told of six feet of snow within her city limits on the day following the English message. Other reports came next, terrible reports that told of deaths, fires, panics, and battles. Edinburgh and Glasgow had succumbed almost simultaneously, one London wire said. A monstrous wall of ice that advanced southward at the rate of about three miles a day crushing everything relentlessly before it, fell upon them and found them bereft of living creatures.

Denmark was the next victim. Copenhagen reports had it that about half a day before the face of the glacier appeared, the thermometer fell very noticeably; this was attended by strong northern winds and a heavy snowfall out of a sky that was as lead. Huge cakes of ice battered themselves together on the waves in the harbor, finally to come to rest in one unbroken layer, jagged and peaked, that covered the water as far as the eye could see. Then like a wolf gone mad with days of hunger, a ragged wall of ice, fully fifty feet high, suddenly came from behind the curtain of falling snow in from the sea and threw itself without mercy upon the doomed city. In one day's time Copenhagen became one with Babylon and Troy, a crushed city under thousands of tons of jagged peaked ice.

London, blazing in the snow-storm, held out stalwartly for nearly two whole days, her final message to the world being a report by wireless that told of three feet of ice in Trafalgar Square. Stories were told later—stories too gruesome to report—of forsaken men and women who waded into the cold waters of the Channel with voices wailing, and arms extended toward the last of the vessels that were moving pitilessly out to sea, braving the huge bergs that were everywhere—of sieve-like boats never heard from again that took to sea their mad human cargoes, who feared the glacier more than they did the deep—of desperate mobs fighting madly, crushing one another on piers and docks, and floating bodies that icy waves cast back upon the shores—of futile last attempts, wild bids for life, huge bonfires built, walls erected, ditches dug to stem the fury from the pole. Stories came of mad fatalists, who died with fanatical eyes looking toward the sky, many cursing their native England that had proved so terrible a death-trap to so vast a number of her sons and daughters. And the background of this picture was a burning city.

GERMANY came next and France followed not far behind her. But from Berlin or Paris, the news was the same. Cold winds, snows, a blizzard, and then a day or two later a huge wall of ice, a moving plateau behind the descending curtain of white, an ice field that seemed to have no end and that mounted higher and higher as it advanced and crushed underneath it five thousand years of civilized labor. Those who had fled to the hill-tops saw the terrible scenes in the valleys below them and some of them survived to tell the tale.

In Asia, after the bleak tundra lands of Siberia had been made short work of, the big, overcrowded cities of northern China were the first to bow before the polar king. Oriental fatalism coupled with the intrinsic secretiveness of the dwellers of the East has kept us from an exact knowledge of what really took place in the Chinese cities when the glacier came. From the few stories that have filtered through and have by now become history, the destruction seemed the same as elsewhere.

Of all our states, Maine was the first victim of the boreal foe. Canada had just been covered, her cities crushed and her eight million population dead or scattered, and all of northern Europe and Asia was one vast ice field when the United States first felt the shock. But the glacial vanguard found a land bereft of humanity, when it crossed the Canadian border and entered Maine. The evening of this same day found me supping at the Dunraven table in the old white mansion on West Eighty-Third Street.

The amateur scientist was jubilant. The formerly inattentive press had not only vindicated him, but had actually thrown themselves at his feet, craving pardon and begging advice. He was the most sought after person in a madman's world and to him, revenge was sweet indeed. "Let 'em freeze" was his favorite phrase.

"Boston is getting colder," my host remarked, his eyes glued to a long telegram. "There is half-a-foot of snow on the Common and more coming down fast. The harbor is frozen in places and the N. Y., N. H., & H. R. R. service has been curtailed due to man-shortage.

"Ha—what's this? Uh, a plea from Chicago to come quick and save their city. 'For God's sake,' it says. So they've pricked up their ears at last and are beginning to listen.

They've thrown aside their scandal sheets and are looking to science for something more than inventions of soda bottles and safety pins, eh? Oh, well, folks, sorry, but I cannot help. I can do no more to keep the glacier off your town than you can. Get out, is my only advice. You had plenty of time to beat it. You were warned months ahead."

ON my way back to the hotel, I encountered a long procession of shouting paraders. Cries to heaven were coming from a hundred vociferous throats. To them, excited Seventh Day Adventists, it was the end of the world, Christ's second coming. On a corner, a bit farther down the street, a rabid, shouting revivalist was exhorting to penitence a shivering crowd, part of which was kneeling in the snow. Across the way from him a Salvation Army group was holding a big throng with music and song. Many of the men were bareheaded and a few excited ones were shouting. Still, farther down, a little elderly lady was standing on the rear of a text-besmeared Ford truck and with tears in her eyes, talked of Armageddon, the end of the world, and of preparedness. A few steps from my hotel an excited young man asked me if I was prepared and then without awaiting an answer, thrust a paper into my hand and hurried away. It was an invitation to hear one Reverend Armitage explain "the true cause of these terrible times that show that worldliness is rewarded only with death, and to tell the results that are soon to come." The world had suddenly awakened to the fact that their worship had been but church-adorning, conventional, and parrot-like lip-service, and now that fear had become their master, like drowning men grasping at straws, they turned toward the unknowable.

AND the snow fell and the sun was never strong enough to melt it and so it became ice and the rivers froze and the seas also, and pushed by its own weight, this became the glacier, and the world shivered in the biting winds that hurried from the ice fields to warmer lands. North and south the tall, icy skyscrapers from the pole lifted their heads and a blizzard-mown plateau of ice stood at their back.

CHAPTER SIX
The Panic

NEW YORK CITY, white with the snow, had dwindled down to a mere half-million population in two months' time. Rioting had abated and no police was necessary to keep in order the foredoomed metropolis. Detroit, Denver, Chicago, Omaha and Philadelphia all reported the same. Silent, dead cities where men and women walked the streets like so many ghosts, as if expecting the fall of the dreaded doom at any moment. Seattle, Portland, and San Francisco felt a bit secure on their warmer Pacific coast, while Los Angeles was boastful and jubilant. The exodus was still going on, the tail end of a gigantic, mad parade. The Dunraven domicile was still the last court of appeals to the ones to whom hope was a thing alive. Once, as I entered its high, wide portal reminiscent of a gateway into some medieval stronghold, I almost collided with the pudgy figure of the little baldheaded city alderman, whom I had remarked before. He apologized meekly and still twitching his derby hat in a nervous manner, hurried down the stairs.

"Damned fool," commented Dunraven, before the little man had time to reach the sidewalk. "What does he think I am? A second Aladdin with a magic lamp? I can't see what he's so excited about. Wants me to engineer a plan, a long line of big furnaces or heaters from coast to coast to melt the glacier as it arrives. What do you think of that for an asinine idea? If they want furnaces let them build furnaces. I'm going where it's warm. This winter climate doesn't quite agree with my gout."

That night I shook his hand at the Mineola air-field.

CLARA was with a maiden aunt in south Texas. Paul was in Panama. I was in cold New York City, a worried man. The periodical with which I was connected and which gave me bread and board was preparing for an aerial voyage to Tampa, Florida, and I, unhappily, was destined to remain in the north and send down the reports of my observations as the glacier advanced. I felt like a lost child in a forest of very tall trees.

Chicago, Denver, Omaha, Philadelphia, Kansas City, and New York felt the chilly grasps of the Sixth Glacier at about the same time. Detroit and Minneapolis had long ago succumbed. The high altitude of the states of the Midwestern plateau did not prove to be a barrier. The Rockies, that tall backbone of the continent, held the glacier back in place for a brief time but soon the oncoming wall of ice merely divided itself upon the mountains' crest and like a huge tidal wave swept away everything in its path. On the fourteenth day of August, a big snowstorm raged over the Atlantic seaboard from the Potomac northward and east from the Appalachians. New York City became as Montana in mid-winter and a curtain of flaky white fell like a milky pall over everything and left behind it a two foot depth of snow. A strong north wind prevailed and the thermometer dropped to eight below the zero mark. The Hudson River was one solid ribbon of ice-covered with twenty-four inches of frozen snow. Two river boats, appearing for all the world like a couple of very squat, white toads in the misty, snowbound distance, were locked fast in the chilly embrace of the frozen stream. From the dock of one of the Hoboken ferries, I was able to make out the dim smoke of a burning town on the Jersey side curl up toward the leaden sky like a gigantic ostrich feather waving in the wind and snow.

THEN one day Nature mocked the barriers that she herself had erected, and crossing the tall Carpathians and the taller Alps, entered the flatlands of southern Europe. The news fell like a crack of doom upon a hopeful mankind and once again there was a stampede of madmen toward the south. The cold Mediterranean Sea became the graveyard of countless unfortunates.

London lay crushed under a thousand feet of ice. Paris was daily awaiting a similar fate. Rome was freezing. Madrid reported fourteen degrees below the zero mark on the same day that the glacier crossed the Alps. Tokyo and Peking were both in the throes of an Arctic blizzard while our own Pacific cities began to fear the worst, despite the warm currents from the tropics.

Day and night I remained within the warm confines of the red brick edifice which housed the offices of the *Scientific Union,* eating and sleeping within arm's length of the improvised wireless set which alone kept me linked with the small portion of the outer world that was unfrozen. However, now that I knew that I too must soon follow, a happy man indeed was I to know that in the shed below a high-powered automobile sled was even now awaiting my disposition.

I think back to those last few terrible days, as I jot down these facts, which I observed, and I can recall how the blizzard grew in its might, how a deep white blanket became hourly ever deeper, and how the final remnant of a stricken five and a half million awaited in fear and silence the crack of doom.

Europe and Asia had ceased to send out their messages of woe. South America and southern Africa, however, continued to tell their tales of the other glacier which came from the south. Once my set received the pitiful S. O. S. call of a Jap fleet of over fifty men of war that had suddenly been caught in a net of ice hills in the region of Sekhelin. But those messages did not last long. In my mind's eye I was able to see fifty ships, big and small, in an ocean full of icebergs struggling vainly and gallantly in the face of their relentless and unconquerable foe. And then came a huge, solid wave that moved slowly yet terribly. When that passed the ships were gone. Only a jagged field of ice remained, immense in its solitude, each peak capped with the snows that were to remain for years and a blizzard played furiously upon its breast.

A last word came from Boston before that old city of patriots went down, a cry of warning. Albany, Buffalo, Cleveland and some other nearby cities kept in hourly touch with me, each one of us exchanging reports. Now the last of the Great Lakes had frozen solid, a motionless body of ice; now Niagara Falls roared no longer, and then Chicago reported the glacier only fifty miles away.

The wind had abated and with it the blizzard died—died venting its fury on the ice-bound land below. Only a steady white stream of falling snow-flakes remained as ushers of the Juggernaut of ice that would come on silent feet and crush everything in its path. I took advantage of the lull and wandering about a bit came in front of the tall Woolworth building, that mammoth tower among mammoth towers. A sudden impulse overtook me and a half hour later I was on its top. Below me stretched a landscape as white as milk, as silent as the grave, while above me the falling snow hid a lead-hued sky. My eyes pierced the curtain of white and dimly made out the snow-covered Statue of Liberty, a forlorn lady, still holding the guiding: light in one bronze hand. The Brooklyn Bridge across the East River appeared like a long white ribbon, losing itself in a distant drift. In the distance and across the frozen Hudson I saw a pink speck and a hazy column of taupe colored smoke that wafted heavenward from it. The town of Paterson was afire.

NIGHT found me safe home again. The snow continued to fall and to deepen the soft, white carpet that was everywhere. A solitary message out of the air broke into my slumbers at about midnight. A confederacy of scattered European nations had established a temporary group capital at Bulawayo in the state of South Rhodesia, Equatorial Africa. Woe unto the poor black man, I thought, the white man has come to stay. With that I went back to bed and a dreamless sleep.

When morning came the snow had stopped falling. But the sky was the color of old, used canvas. The thermometer stood at twenty degrees below the zero mark and a strong north wind was blowing. No more messages came from Albany, Rochester, or Buffalo. The northern part of the state was silent. During breakfast Chicago spoke two words: "It's here."

CHAPTER SEVEN
New York City under the Ice

FOR the sixth time since life on earth first sprang into existence in the torrid mud seas of its early Paleozoic days, the polar ice was slowly coming down again, upon the unsuspecting world, crushing everything in its frozen path. Peace and quiet reigned save for our ubiquitous bickerings, such petty affairs in this grand scheme of things, and then came the glacier. Once again Nature had won and was even now gathering in the stakes; cruelly, relentlessly.

UNDER the cover of the ebony of a starless night, like a wolf upon a sheep fold, silently came the glacier upon fearful

New York City. Only the noon before a fur-clad individual, bewhiskered and very excited, a telegraph operator from Poughkeepsie; dropped in to see me. He had stuck valiantly to his post to the last, and left only a few hours before the ice came behind a curtain of storm. I welcomed him heartily, for he was the first human being that I had seen in many a day. He lingered only a few minutes, told me in an excited voice that the glacier was even now battering at the portals of the city, and then with a hasty adieu, commenced his long sled journey to the southlands. An hour later I, too, was speeding across the snow covered, lifeless Jersey plains.

Near Trenton I encountered a group of government aviators on observation duty and a wild idea entered my head. Anyhow, I was still a reporter, a representative of a periodical, put here on the scenes of disaster to observe and report the transpiring events. Why should I not get one last glimpse of the big metropolis, which for over a quarter of a century had been hearth and home to me, the place which had harbored my loves, my hates, my hopes? I must defy this relentless boreal fury. Ye gods, what a scoop! What a headliner! And all my own.

I went up in the airplane. The sky was low and leaden, a dull unbroken canopy of grey clouds that obscured the blue of the firmament, but the snow on the ground below was as a mirror and thus there was no dearth of light. New York City lay beneath me swaying to and fro as the plane wavered in the gale, an octopus of a city, milk-white, tomb-like. Everything was quiet and dead.

We hovered a little over a thousand feet above the city. I could clearly make out each individual building below me. In the distant north snow was falling. It was the curtain behind which the ice wall slunk. The long, thread-like, streets below bobbed up and down before me as my aerial charge, like a light craft on a choppy sea, bounced about in midair. I did not dare venture too far into the teeth of the gale. I had to be satisfied to watch it from a safe distance as it drove before its fury huge clouds of snow. I saw the havoc of the wind beneath me. I saw the leaden mantle of the sky above me, and to the north of me the curtain of snow. Even as I looked this curtain seemed to be rent asunder. And then, like the high prow of some Cyclopean ship, the icy nose of the glacier tore through the storm. Into the residential part of the city it tore—with the roar of a thousand Niagaras, the fury of a thousand miles, and before its might man's handicraft gave way and was crushed and plowed under by ice.

IT was a wonderful and terrible sight. A solid mass of glittering, scintillating ice, a huge chilling ploughshare nearly one hundred feet high that bore behind it the weight of a frozen continent, cut a wide gap into the scene below and house after house, block after block was hopelessly shattered. In an echelon formation, like the battle-phalanx of Alexander's conquering Greeks, it paved a way for the newest ice age. Somewhere far in the rear, perhaps hundreds of miles behind, a grand upheaval must undoubtedly have taken place and hurled suddenly and unexpectedly upon its wretched victim this pointed mass that was supposed to come in a more leisurely fashion, a huge field of ice that rose in height as it stretched northward, peak after peak, vale after vale, and lost itself in the mist of the falling snow. With the speed of an express train it burst out of the curtain that fell thickly from the massed, gray clouds. The glacier that so far had advanced so slowly and had behaved so well had suddenly burst its gyves and spread rapid destruction in its wake. A second sufficed it to cross the narrow Harlem River and fix itself on the main part of the gigantic city. Then through the once thickly populated heart of Gotham, it swiftly swept, spreading a landscape of tall, spired peaks white with freshly fallen snow, crushing, tearing, rending asunder. Like the prow of a speed-boat the tall apex of the phalanx struck the congested, world famous business district of New York. For one awful moment the huge buildings, marvels of the engineers' genius, held their own nobly. Then they wavered a bit, some of the exterior masonry coverings fell off and buried themselves in the three feet deep snow on the ground below and exposed the steel girder skeleton framework from underneath the brick and stone, then as a hundred-billion tons of ice pressed irresistibly forward, the big edifices crumpled up and became one with the past. One big, slender tower, a finger of steel and stone pointing at the sky, broke into two and fell. A row of huge office buildings, mighty structures of concrete and steel, were brushed helplessly to one side and crushed one upon the other as the ice advanced. The sturdy Municipal Building, hardiest of them all, valiantly held its head high until one side of the icy echelon brushed along it, tearing away much of its lower concrete. Huge pieces of ice broke off the main body of the cold plow-share and piled themselves up talus-like, almost to one half of the height of the tall edifice. Even when the greater part of one wall was already gone, steel-work and all, and the building itself was slanting awry, the ice continued to pile up around. Still it stood. And then it was pushed to one side, indifferently, just as some obtrusive clod of earth is pushed out of the path by a plow. For a moment the gigantic structure struggled as though it were a living thing. From a bird's-eye-view, it seemed a huge, antediluvian, unearthly living thing. Uprooted from its solid base of deeply sunk caissons, falling to pieces bit by bit, I watched it as it traveled for a hundred yards or more with the swiftly moving ice prow of the glacier, a skeleton of a building, shattering its smaller neighbors in its final bid for existence. Its naked dome toppled grotesquely to one side like a drunkard's hat. Then like a house of cards it fell to pieces; hundreds of tons of steel and stone. But the glacier heeded nothing. It merely moved on, bayward, southward, a jagged field of ice that stretched for miles toward the pole. It brushed the tall Statue of Liberty to one side, and threw it heavily into the ice-covered water, hurling huge cakes of ice high into the air, and then lifted little Bedlo's Island bodily out of the bay. It tore the long bridges, from their stony foundations and then crushed them to pieces underneath its icy feet. New York City had become one with Nineveh and the hoariest of pasts in fifteen minutes. In the distance and toward the north the snow still fell.

A RIGID Arctic winter had set in. The sun shone feebly, a weak spot of light in an opaque sky. No Aurora told of the sunrise, no gory skies afire told of the death of day. A brazen sky alone roofed the northern world, stretching from one horizon to the other.

We flew along the ice-bound coast, through the white state of New Jersey, over Delaware, and high above snow-bound Maryland. On the land below us the glacier never resting, advanced more slowly now. On the sea great cliffs of ice, hundreds of feet high and as irregular as the waves that made them and thick with snow, faced the rolling waters and occasionally shed their giant bergs seaward-tall peaks with hoary heads that touched the gray canopy that blanketed the sky as they rode southward on the waves' crest. Here and there, on the whiteness below us lay motionless black spots, those of the retreating army that were unable to carry on. At one place a huge Red Cross sign, darkly outlined in the snow, told of succor and mercy, an outpost harbinger of solace in a land which knew of it but faintly. Once we passed low over a straggling caravan, a tail end of a mad stampede, hurrying before the icy lash of Nature as only those hurry, who know well that Death is the pacemaker. We flew low over

Baltimore, deeply covered with snow, a mute city, silent and deserted, awaiting the doom of the inevitable.

The snow held sway as far south as Washington, D. C. In the Potomac huge cakes of ice, floated languidly while on its southern shore a small steamer was stranded and afire. The big Capitol building, a squat, milky monster, merged its whiteness with that of the snow. I saw the first sunshine in many a day in this doomed capital city of a scattered nation, a welcome orb that reflected its light on the white mirror beneath it and played havoc with the eyes.

We landed in Richmond, Virginia's fair capital, a city as old as the south—now a Richmond overcrowded with madmen. Festered with disease, hunger, and crime, with a homeless, terror-stricken populace, it awaited the glacier's coming sedately and with dignity, like an aristocrat.

Galveston harbor was a sea of naked masts, long, skinny fingers pointing arrow-like to the sky, like so many dead and scorched pine-trunks after a forest fire. Clara was in Galveston, living with a maiden aunt. Her father was in northern Mexico busy within the depths of his ruins. For my part our meeting was a happy one, though what impression my month's growth of beard and my unkempt person made on the girl, I could not say.

Washington went to her icy doom five days after New York City had met the same fate. It did not go with the sudden unexpected onrush of a sea of ice that wrote "finis" to the three-hundred year history of the greater city; it went slowly, like a huge pachyderm pushing its way through a forest of tender saplings, irresistibly and yet without concern. The huge Capitol torn from its age old base, was pushed along for about a mile by a fifty feet high ice wall, crumpling to pieces as it went, its magnificent cupola falling to the ground at one half of that distance; and finally the thick masonry gave way and fell to pieces before the weight and ponderosity of the glacier.

The tall Washington Monument, so eyewitnesses claim, broke into three pieces at the first impact and buried each piece in the deep snow at its feet.

I HAD scarcely been in Galveston for two days when an order from the new office of the *Scientific News* at Tampa reached me. I was to be there as soon as possible. A quarter of an hour later I was at Clara's house again for another farewell. Paul was there too, fresh from Panama, a merry sunburnt Paul, eager and furtive—in contrast to my haggard, care-worn self. He was endeavoring to induce Clara and her aunt to return with him to the tropics, now, alas, grown very temperate, indeed. I was a very happy man when I heard them refuse.

CHAPTER EIGHT
"Bender, We Must Do Something"

ONCE again I was looking down upon a sparsely covered pink scalp immediately above a pair of narrow shoulders.

"Have a chair, Bender," said the little editor wearily. Undoubtedly he had been up late the night before. "Had a jolly cold time in New York, didn't you? Your story was excellent. Congratulations. You've certainly got the stuff in you and if the glacier doesn't force us back into the pre-Neolithic clays I prophesy a great future for you. Mark my words."

I answered something or other in reply, almost inaudibly—a thanks, I believe. He seemed not to hear me.

"The world is panic stricken, Bender," he continued. "I too am beginning to see only the worst. To me it is the end. Yes, Bender, the finish. The last chapter of our civilization has been written and the Grand Author is even now putting the period in the final line—the book is complete and finished. Yes, Bender, we must do something; something to stop the ice. Do you think old Dunraven could help? A real big wall, a deep ditch, perhaps. A billion hands are ready to help. The Italians, so I hear, are taking advantage of the internal volcanic heat with which their little peninsula home is at one time blessed and cursed.

"We ought to be out of the frigid area soon. Good Lord, it can't last forever, and once out, the ice will go quick. The last glacier, if all indications are true, did not go farther south than Ohio and on this I rest much hope. It is not the thought that the glacier will cover up the entire surface of the globe that puts fear into my heart and makes me cry dismally that all is lost. It is the sadly terrible sight of humanity wiping itself out. When the sun shines again someday and we are free of the icy marauders from the poles, what a tiny wretched remnant will be saved. It will hardly be worth saving."

He paused for a moment and regarded me, but noting that I made no comments, continued.

"You see, Bender, it's like this. So long as we are in the cold belt, the sun's heat is nil, for the atmosphere no longer holds the heat. The seas and the inland waters freeze, and expanding, spread the frigid temperature. Like a snowball growing bigger and bigger as it rolls down-hill, the glacier feeds on itself as it goes, using its victims to garner in more. There is little news from Europe now. Spain and France both breathed their last a week ago; thousands perished on the ice sea which was once the Mediterranean. Italy is still holding out in her lowlands, but it is only a question of time. Greece is hit, though Turkey, as far as I know now, is still untouched, while Egypt has had its first snow-storm in its sixty centuries of history. A white night-cap of ice and snow rests on the top of the world and is growing bigger every day. Yes, Bender, we must do something."

THE Himalayas proved to be no barriers. The glacier went through them like a hot knife through butter, tearing everything to pieces as it went. I pictured it in my mind's eye, the tall Indo-Chinese range, majestic, serene, invincible, defiant of time and of element, those hoary Asiatic pillars of the blue firmament of the Far East bowing down before the polar foe. Nature's mightiest rampart scaled at last and the sunny plains below at the mercy of the ice. Like a cinema display, a scene that in reality took weeks to enact, passed in a rapid review before my mental eye. I saw the slow advance of the tall ice wall behind the curtain of falling snow. Siberia long ago conquered, China just surrendered, slowly, ponderously, a living, relentless entity twenty-thousand miles long, a thousand billion tons behind it. I saw it creep, hour by hour, into the arid foot-hills of the skyscraping mountain chain, swallow them overnight, and then push farther on. I saw it pile itself high over the deepest of chasms and the widest of gorges, and at the feet of the tallest peaks as the king of mountain ranges made its final stand. I saw it creep up slowly, through one mountain pass, another, into a valley and then swiftly across a plain, hurling itself forward with the weight of a world behind it, surrounding giant peak after giant peak like a living, crawling, many-armed hydra, mercilessly crushing the mountain villages that stood in its way. I saw the fight on the timberline as the ice arose, the big pines giving way like so much brushwood, up, up, until only the tallest peaks remained above the ice, tiny, peaked islands covered with snow and losing themselves in a gray blanket of clouds.

North Texas and the mid-west plateau states felt the grip of the glacier at about the same time that Salt Lake City did. Big bergs floated down the Mississippi, and jamming into one solid mass, made of the Father of Waters a river of ice. Those refugees who had only so recently been driven to seek newer homes in the southlands were beginning to feel uneasy again.

On the first day of October Los Angeles was unanimously decided on as the capital of the United States. It snowed many inches deep that day all along the Pacific coast as far south as the Mexican border; nevertheless the Los Angelites turned out en masse to welcome the nation's noblest.

OF course the glacier's advance was not a matter of speed, except in the case of the destruction of New York City, whose unlucky remnant of once proud millions died in a trap suddenly sprung. Ordinarily the ice fields moved toward the corpulent equator of the earth at the rate of about five miles a day, ample time for flight, though it would take longer in mountainous regions.

The admixture of homeless peoples who pressed madly into the iceless places of the world had very unwisely sought the seasides and the big cities instead of the more open plains and the jungle's almost unlimited terrains. The gregariousness of the herd animal, of which man too is a species, manifested itself in overcrowded cities where death, disease, and vice was rife. Others, however, were made of sterner stuff. Tent cities and long, even avenues of hastily constructed shanties sprang tip as if by the rub of an Aladdin's lamp in valleys; in forests, and by the brinks of rivers and seas. These were the nuclei of newer nations to come. Forests were cleared and streams bridged, and prairies once given over entirely to wild grasses and wilder winds were plowed and tilled. Everything was done to cover freezing bodies and fill hungry mouths. At first showing signs of belligerency, the countries of the tropics, however, soon bowed before the inevitable, and powerless in the face of a billion desperate invaders either offered aid or assumed an indifference that verged on fatalism. It soon became a case of nations within nations, immense ghettos in foreign lands. Temporary seats of governments were erected and armed vigilantes maintained order without scruple or hesitation. Strict laws rivaling those of Lycurgus of ancient history were the immediate and natural offspring of those terrible times and death was the penalty for infringement. People desperately combated the baser elements of man which come to the surface when he is scared or otherwise caught unawares.

CHAPTER NINE
The World at Bay

THE tall arboreal mammoths of our northwestern woods bowed before the titanic fields of ice, yet they had dared Nature's grimmest dangers for a half-score of centuries. California was invaded; the tall Sierra Nevadas were traversed by the glacier, and the southern deserts became its bed. And still the northern fury—kept coming on—creeping slowly, mile by mile. One day Tokyo sent a message that all was over. The next day Manila had a snow-storm.

On this side of the globe a wedge-shaped world of ice, like the prow of a Cyclopean ship, five thousand, miles long, held in its grasp the biggest part of the land. Its point was north Texas, high and cold, and thence it ran in a more or less irregular line as far north as San Francisco on the west coast and northeast as far as the Virginia hills. South of it was a cold land of refugees driven from their homes. North of it a colder land of boreal storms. The Los Angeles vicinity was fast becoming an Arctic country and the prospects of hunting a newer national capital were becoming more imminent daily. Gray clouds hid the one time azure sky of the California city and huge ice cakes covered her distant harbor. For one solid week the snow never ceased to fall and the streets were carpeted with a foot of soft, white flakes. Her huge population, swelled to overflowing by the influx of a myriad of homeless ones, was moving desertward hour by hour. Atlanta received her baptism of ice simultaneously with San Francisco and both natives and fugitives suddenly quit their erstwhile bellicose desires and became an army of stragglers toward the Gulf.

In Europe, Rome and Madrid were both under the glacier. Athens was a deserted city in the power of a raging blizzard solemnly awaiting an icy death. Practically all of Europe was covered before the Hellenes were reached. Constantinople was full of refugees and very cold. Cairo had been burning for a week, and Fez, Tuns, and Algiers were shambles. Buluways was made the temporary capital of the nascent European Confederacy, extending its boundaries, and primeval jungle and native bamboo village had to give way. Fighting with the blacks was a daily affair and the prey-birds of the air feasted and gorged well on human flesh.

From Asia came no news. India was one vast uninterrupted battlefield where yellow man and brown fought tooth and claw, one to find a haven from the glacier's cruel menace, the other to hold back from hearth and home a Mongol tide. The islands of the South Seas proved hell-holes for millions. Japan alone showed any signs of sanity. She took possession of the Philippines, Hawaii and Guam and moved the stricken remnant of the Mikado's population there. The little island kingdom of the rising sun had proved to be like Britain on the globe's opposite side, a death-trap to her overcrowded millions. New Zealand was under and Australia was breathing her last. Sydney and Melbourne both reported snow while Ballarat was covered with ice. The southern glacier was coming to meet its northern ally; the jaws of the vise were closing.

ONE day I found a letter awaiting me at the new office of the *Scientific News*. In places the postal service was still in existence. The envelope bore the stamp of Mexico and even before I opened it the neat, almost girlish hand apprised me of the fact that the writer was none other than my scientifically inclined friend. He was very brief. A few lines (light green ink on pink paper, scented!), he thought, would suffice to tell me that he was at present at the site of his archeological "find" near Magdalena. He had discovered something new and desired my immediate presence. "Just a few lines for your sheet that will do it good," he wrote. And "I know that they'll allow me no more." He passed over the glacier simply by stating that he thought he had a remedy. Clara, he mentioned, was in Mexico City.

The next day I started toward Mexico and two days later was in Magdalena, a city of the living dead, where a million starving men and women eyed one another greedily, in constant fear that someone might want a bite to eat. Martial law reigned with an iron hand, a Mexican martial law that was bereft of scruples and knew how to be swift. A food-issue rule had been in existence for a long time and hoarders were shot. Dead bodies were daily carted out to the sandy edge of the overgrown town and there cremated. A pair of gibbets, gruesome reminders of the power of the law, graced the main plaza, and daily they bore the bitterest of fruits. Armed soldiers, with bayonets fixed, guarded the streets and lurked in every ally, so that Magdalena was akin to a military post or an invaded city. The laws were of iron and it was necessary that it should be so.

Now as I write reviewing those awful days, so hectic and eventful, and so terrible, it seems to me like some bad dream that existed only in the imagination. An ancient ruin found by a rich old man with a penchant toward science, a warning never heeded, the first cries of distress, two huge glaciers coming relentlessly, like the two jaws of a vise, from the two poles, a stampede of scared humans made desperate by their plight, a world of fugitives, and a world of ice and storms.

Today, in retrospect, it appears more like a nightmare of many years ago than the terrible reality that it really was. I recall the day upon which I arrived in Magdalena and immediately sought Stephen Dunraven. An hour later I found him in a dirty khaki-tent which evidently had seen better days, at the edge of the town, distant from the turmoil of humanity. The little Jap serving man, immobile as ever, was still at his elbow, bowing and very polite, just as he had been before.

"How are you, Bender?" Dunraven greeted me in the gruff tone of a "bucko" second-mate ordering a surly sailor aloft. A hearty handshake gave immediate lie to the comparison. "Sit down next to me on this cot. Easy, it's broke. Ido, something to drink."

IDO entered with hot tea and rum, a fit beverage for such a cold climate.

"I've hopes for the best," continued my host, "but of that later. At present, I have something else for you and the readers of the *Scientific News*. First, we shall proceed to the ruins. Next, you shall wire enough to Tampa to fill a page or two of your magazine. I hope old Hillsboro will be contrite enough to devote that much to the cause of a very humble dilettante of science with a foolish paleontological twist of mind. Paul is here and I will endeavor to talk him into the notion of driving us over to the digging, which, I must confess, he is never overeager to do."

I trudged alongside of him in silence and nodded to Paul as I took the back seat of a mud beplastered sedan of a more or less ancient vintage. The corpulent amateur-scientist sat down heavily beside me saying that a back seat was more comfortable. I smiled inwardly as I thought of his fondness for me as a good listener.

The sun was already reddening the western skyline, broken in a hundred places by hog-back peaks, when we started for the huge excavation. The trip would last four or five hours and it would be dark by the time we arrived. We must wait there overnight and only on the morrow delve into the secrets of the mystery city of the past.

Stephen Dunraven was a veritable fountain of words. Today his topic was glaciers and he began to talk the moment that Paul threw in the car's clutch and a noisy grating told that we were off. I was a very interested listener.

"The first ice age," he told me, "came many millions of years ago during the long, fiery youth of our little globe, the Archeozoic, which was bereft of all life, eons before the waters swarmed with life.

"Then came the second ice age at the beginning of the Paleozoic, when the world still had summers from pole to pole as the fossil corals found in the frigid zones mutely tell us. The globe was vast swamp and a vaster sea, and sponges, jelly-fish, and star-fish were all alone in life. Land was at a premium, hence there was no land-life.

"And from then on each geological era had an ice age that lasted for a million years and was divided into periods of glaciation as we passed through the frigid belt, only to pass through it again in another one hundred some odd thousand years. Thus five or six times during each ice age the glaciers from the two poles would come north and south. Then would come eons when all would be iceless and summer again as our little solar groups would vagabond through spaces where no frigid belt played its pranks. And all the time our terrestrial orb was slowly cooling off to make a home for humanity possible, until someday the fatal journey through the frigid belt would come and mark a 'finis' to it all, drawing a curtain of eternity on this short, tragic drama of terrestrial life.

"Immense coal-forests of cycads and giant forms, the sole, vegetation of the Carbonaceous Period, absorbed much of the carbon dioxide of the then thick atmosphere of ·our earth and helped pave a way for the ice. And then when the glacier came, these tender trees died; ages later upheavals covered and buried them under the newer lands, and today they are our coal-mines. Yes, the coal that you now burn in your furnace was nothing more than carbon dioxide and sunshine in the Jurassic air.

"AS there were immense forests in those days so too there were immense beasts, monstrous gargoyle-visaged, brainless behemoths, such as opium eaters see in opium dreams, and then when the first cold days came fast upon the heels of the warm and murky Coal Age they slew these dragons and made the existence of man possible on the surface of the earth. Yes, Bender, it is a paradox, but the ice ages had helped mankind and its advent toward a civilized life by allowing only the fittest to survive their terrible rigors. Nature slew the giant beasts with whom the poor weaponless primitive man would never have been able to compete, thinned the air for his tenderer lungs, and destroyed the huge miasmatic plants to make room for his forests and plains. Then again, the last ice age socialized him, the primordial and savage one, and made him gregarious. It was around the fires built for warmth and in the caves sought for wind-breaks that home-life and clan-life began. In truth the glacier took the ape off the tree-tops and setting him on his hind legs made a man. On the ground, he had to use his brain and thus the brain developed, and in time the hunted one became the hunter and the master of the world. It was just another way that Nature had of keeping up the nobler race. That is just what the Grand Gardener is doing today.

"And yet the ice ages grow severer and longer each time. This one is merely a foretaste of the endless cold that is to come and which one day shall cover all, and leave our little globe a cold, lifeless orb hurtling through space. Our terrestrial divisions of temperature into torrid, temperate, and frigid zones are very recent, for it was only at the end of the Cretaceous or Chalk Period that these divisions began. Before that all was summer the year round. No, I do not think that we shall ever regain the temperatures of those yester-eons of yore. Cold days have followed each ice age and our little orb is steadily cooling down. In time an eternal winter shall take the place of the eternal summer, between which two our little span of humanity is just a transitive period of springtime weather.

"A great average fall of temperature is not necessary to an ice age. Of course, there is a sudden and enormous drop as the first wall of ice hits, heralded in by the storm due to a mass of clouds that the ice is pushing before it, congealed particles of moisture in the atmosphere. I would not be one whit surprised to find human beings even now alive on the jagged back of the moving fields of ice, maybe entire settlements of overtaken fugitives which the glacier had spared for a grimmer fate and would not release. Igloo villages may have sprung up where cities once had stood. This is no impossibility."

"A pretty dismal picture," I interrupted with a sardonic smile. "Anything else?"

"Oh yes, one thing more. A large part of the seas solidify and thus there are no tides. Some even fear an increase of the earth's rotation because of the lack of this tidal friction."

CHAPTER TEN
Here Stood a Mighty City Once

AROUND the ruins a camp had sprung. Men, women and children were everywhere. Shifty-eyed scavengers, with pinched faces, were made into human hyenas almost overnight, and fearless beggars lurked in the shadowy doorways of hovels or walked stealthily in the slush of the narrow streets. Whites, dark peons, and dark, full-blooded Indians with tattered clothes elbowed one another on the noisy, narrow streets.

"Quite a mob," Paul remarked as he zigzagged his honking car through their midst, and they gave way reluctantly to the asthmatic sedan. "I wish they wouldn't clog up these narrow streets so much."

A quarter of an hour later we were challenged by a dark-skinned rifleman and five minutes later we were on our way into the earth's interior.

HERE stood a mighty city once. Now it was being recaptured from time and decay with its chronicles of the dead eons. It had braved the wrath of time and decay. The tall octagon-shaped tower, which the amateur scientist had so raved about, stood there, a molded pillar of reddish brown, tall, silent, and austere, like a captured prince, among some tiny comrades.

Everywhere before our eyes, north, east, south and west ran long straight, narrow streets, reminiscent of Chinese cities. Scantily clothed working men, some brown, some white, appeared like an army of busy ants in the bottom of a huge pit. Ancient walls, battered by time and hoary with age, saw their first daylight in many a dark century as pick, shovel and crowbar brought them forth to vision. Beside me stood the founder of it all, Stephen Dunraven, the avatist of a Napoleon and a scientific Bedouin.

An old man advanced to meet us, dust-covered, feeble of gait, snow-white of beard, a very old man who appeared as if he long ago had forgotten to answer the endless roll-call of Time—a very imposing old man.

"Professor von Moritz, from Munich," Paul was whispering in my ear, and a moment later the aged savant confronted us, panting like an asthmatic after a severe spasm.

"Ach, so it is you," he chortled after a somewhat lengthy scrutiny of the amateur paleontologist. "It's so good to see you." His voice was cracked and very low.

We shook hands, his was a cracked and withered hand, like a tiny ancient parchment.

"Wonderful, wonderful," ejaculated the little German, "a lost city of the people who lived in the morning of the world."

I allowed my eyes to turn sideways and gaze at the bulky figure of my host, the amateur scientist and ex-millionaire traction king, who had lost his all, a monarch's ransom, under a mile of ice. He was jubilant.

The diminutive scholar from Munich was talking. "What a strange world this is," he philosophized in a low, squeaky tone, "what a strange world. Civilizations upon civilizations. First spiders and then men. God alone knows what was before the arachnidia.

"Spiders built this city, Bender," the paleontologist broke in abruptly. "Huge spiders, civilized arachnidia. They used us as their slaves, or rather beasts of burden. Of course, by us, I mean the early dawn man, the Pithecanthropus, who was more ape than man, with big teeth and little brain.

"Yes, the professor is right. Civilizations over civilizations—and who can truly say for how far back. Rational mammalia today, only a higher type of ape, rational bugs in a yester-eon. Rational what next? Nothing lasts in Nature. Everything goes to make room for others born of the already used material. It's just like a man with a mass of clay. He must destroy the form he just made before he can make another, a better one, perhaps, and so on *ad infinitum*. Why? Who can say? And, like the fate of these spider people, our two-legged forms, too, shall go, for man is by no means the *ne plus ultra* of life and creation. He is just the beginning of something which our feeble minds cannot comprehend.

"These spiders were too weak to withstand the rigors of the glacier very long, though they did survive long enough to record it and give posterity a warning of a sixth catastrophe, to come. Little did they realize at that time the kind of posterity that would follow and become humanized—almost Ho-hum. *Sic transit gloria mundi.* Thus passes away earthly glory. Just as if our horses and mules a million years from now were to become noble enough to erect cities and organize civilizations."

We had by now reached the base of the tall brick tower, labor of unwilling hands many years ago. A tousled-headed man in very dirty overalls came forward to meet us.

"Mr. Brooks has been waiting for you all day yesterday," he addressed Stephen Dunraven. "He says that he is finished with the washing of the big iron tablet, the one with the hole on top."

"Good boy, Frank. I'll find Brooks soon. He can't be far away. How about that sub-cellar? Is it clear?"

"All clear, sir."

"Anything new?"

"No, nothing."

And with this much the overalled one lingered a bit, but then, upon seeing that no more attention was being paid to him, he turned around and walked away.

MR. BROOKS turned out to be a tall, thin, wry-faced individual and the possessor of a rather shrill voice. He wore a much-abused leather jerkin, like the kind used among the truck drivers and teamsters. His head was long and bald and his age must certainly have hovered in the neighborhood of fifty. Before the Sixth Glacier had driven him to the south and safety, he had been a professor of chemistry in a large mid-western university.

Archeology, however, was his pet hobby, and he had to his credit one or two brochures that dealt with the civilizations of the ancient races. He himself appeared to be almost like a mummy that had suddenly been by some kind of black magic, miraculously brought back to life. He seemed to be fresh from the case. At present he was in charge of a crew of laborers, all of them busy with rags, chemicals and chisels, bringing forth to light and to knowledge, the lore upon the metallic and stone pages of the history books of the spider peoples, whose culture had once upon a time lingered here.

"Morning folks," was the way in which he greeted us. Then, turning toward Stephen Dunraven, "It's done."

"Good. Where is it?"

"Right here, I'll lead the way." And with that he moved ahead of us with almost elephantine dignity, such a contrast to his worn, cowhide vest.

Engraved on a huge plate of iron was the picture of a spider. He was performing some sort of rite on a low altar upon which lay a monkey-visaged man. He was not the kind of a spider that you or I would have expected to see. Imagine, if you can, a flat, oval body, almost human in its upright position, standing erect on four long, thin legs. A grotesque head was popped, almost neckless, upon this oval ball—a gargoyle head out of a hashish-eater's dream. A series of huge eyes, Argus-like, a blunt nose, a cavernous Gargantuan mouth, and a pair of long, delicate mandibles, were all parts of his head. Four long arms, as long and as slender as were the legs, protruding from the oval beneath the head. Judging by the sacrificed troglodyte, the spider must have been at least three feet tall, a smooth-skinned arachnid, at one time Nature's highest creation on our little orb.

"Funny little fellow, with that big body and that tiny head. Wonder what he ever did to get that big half-man, half-monkey brute to obey him?" It was Paul's voice.

"Brains, brains;" answered the little Teuton scholar hastily. "Brains, my dear sir. The ancient predecessor of man lacked them. He was more animal than he was human. Just took at that frontal slope on his head. Like an orangutan, eh? Almost forty-five degrees. And these spiders. They were of a noble race, even if only arachnidia. Astronomers, mathematicians."

We never noticed the arrival of the newcomer, a short, fat, middle-aged Mexican, whose lighter complexion showed him to be a caballero, bereft of Indian or Negroid blood. His bearing was military, as was his tattered uniform. He stopped short a few feet from us, clicked his heels together with a resounding smack, and saluted. A few minutes of low conversation with Stephen Dunraven and he was leading our little group away from the age-old ruins and out of the buried city.

IT was evening; the low, uneven horizon of the west was gory with a desert sunset. From the arid hills, purple in the distance, and the haze, came the buzz of a million refugees, like disturbed hornets around their nest, and then the moon arose and the stars came out and the landscape below was caught in an atmosphere of pale light. Like a wisp of hazy smoke from an unseen fire, a cloudlet floated across the sea of ink above us, radiant in the golden glow of the full moon, for the moon shines golden on the desert. We were driving home and the cold wind added no comfort to the ride.

"Only one way," Stephen Dunraven was saying in English to the fat Mexican official. "Heat her up good and plenty. I've got a scheme. Have it already figured out on black and white in my tent. Step on it a bit, Paul; we'll soon be there and then over hot coffee out of tin cups…" (Ido had learned to make excellent coffee) "…we'll talk things over."

IT was four hours later. Stephen Dunraven was talking. The scene was the crowded interior of his ancient khaki tent.

"Yes, gentlemen, the world is at bay. All of us are away. We'll have to tear down these artificial barriers of creed, caste and nationality and fight Nature, the one real foe. Here…" He slammed a walrus-flapper of a hand heavily down on some blueprints, almost upsetting four cups of coffee, "…are the plans of a jetty, a jetty that shall make history and have much to say and do when the time comes to fight the ice. What I propose, gentlemen, is that we erect a number of huge sea walls anywhere along the African and South American coasts, where the warm equatorial ocean currents gather their torrid waters on their journey to the north. It was this same current returning from the frigid, ice-infected seas around the pole, laden with the chilling waters of the Arctic Ocean, that gave our own Atlantic seaboard, a land on one level with India, snows in the winter and frosts in the fall, and during the late springtimes, when the northlands thawed, it brought along on its crest, as it returned to the south again, the huge bergs of ice which proved a Nemesis to many a noble ship. And this gulf stream still flows, gentlemen; it still flows under the ice. It still continues to bring down the colder waters from beyond the Arctic Circle and return to the pole with what little warm water the tropics can yield now. That is the reason why London, far above the latitude of New York City, received the blast of cold only a little while before the huge American metropolis did, that was also the reason why the aerial observers, with whom I am even now in touch, are able to report a concave dent, the huge sea of ice—hills that only a few months, ago were the North Atlantic Ocean. Here the warm current of the northward-bound gulf stream pushes itself into the gigantic wall of ice.

"And there are water currents just like this one in the Atlantic Ocean south of us and in the Pacific on the other side. My proposition then would be to build a series of jetties of huge sea-walls and with each of these walls a very powerful electric heating appliance of some kind to heat the current as it goes north, and so on in relays more and more as the ice gives way, and then watch out for the icebergs heading south and the flooded lowlands. A Central African jetty will swerve the huge equatorial current, which is caused by trade winds from the east. Its boundaries are shifting ones, from its southeasterly course direct toward the north, where it will conjoin with our own Gulf Stream, which in truth is a part of it, and receiving warm-overs from a string of smaller jetties and their electric heaters, will finally reach the big jetty or sea-wall near Cuba, which then will tend to swerve it nearer to our own Atlantic coast as it journeys toward Europe, only to turn again in the far north and come south, frigid and frost-laden, from Labrador. I recognize the magnitude, gentlemen, of this monstrous undertaking which will require men, money and time galore. Of course, as we stand today, the ice has practically stopped and the jaws of the vice are still many miles apart; nevertheless it is still here and who can say how long it will stay when the interstellar zone of frigidity shall be passed through. The world is at bay. It is our one chance to strike."

With all attention on the speaker, who in his enthusiasm had risen to his feet, we had allowed our coffee to become cold. His words had brought us a newer springtime, a newer dawn. In my mind's eye I was building jetties, huge sea walls, everywhere, and the tropical currents, superheated in relays by huge electric coils, went north, tore asunder the hills of ice and snow, sending down as proofs the gigantic bergs of ice, and reclaimed again the homes of mankind.

CHAPTER ELEVEN
The Building of the Jetty

LOS ANGELES met its fate, an empty city, on the first day of the new year. It required five whole days for the wall of ice to pass from one end of the Californian metropolis to the other, no longer a fifty feet high advance guard of the glacier, relentless, irresistible, but a slow river of ice that had wasted all of its fury in the dreadful deeds of the past. It came very slowly and failed to crush the biggest of the buildings and covered but slightly the west coast city's deserted streets. The Sixth Glacier had already spent itself and could go no further. It stood defiant on a pair of twenty thousand mile long battle lines, a mile deep and with a jagged, icy army of reserves at its back. And now it was man's turn to strike.

Of course, the jetties would be but temporary—a much-needed relief until the last outer fringe of the frigid belt was passed, the sun's heat came down upon us as strong as of yore, and the ice receded to its polar home. Then man would come into his own again. Then, too, as the warm water currents could be only on the oceans, these and the coast lands alone would be benefitted. The millions of square miles of inland plateau, high above the level of the sea, would never be affected and must remain realms of snow and ice, a waif of the boreal lords, until the happy time would come when the sun with its string of little balls shall be in the icy grip of the frigid belt no longer.

The cities, the towns and the hamlets that even now lay crushed and scattered under the shroud of white, were to us lost forevermore. When the ice will have gone and left them uncovered to sunshine once more, only the stoutest of foundations would remain to show where mankind fought with its back to the wall against this icy lash of Nature that spared neither young nor old. Fifty centuries of toil are lost to us forever. We must start all over again, gather the remnants that the glacier spared and erect better houses out of the scattered brick.

Already happy wires were coming from everywhere, wherever the brave outpost watchmen of man's stand before the glacier were posted, that the ice had halted on its marauding errands north and south. The huge jaws of the vise had failed to crush us completely. Part of the world was safe, at any rate, and even if the sun did shine down upon it through a frigid veil, and where sago and coco palm once flourished was now the home of cold winds and frosty nights, there was ample space for every man, woman and child to start life all over again.

Mexico City became the newest of world capitals. As Bulawayo in the State of Rhodesia, Equatorial Africa represented the headquarters of the peoples of Europe, and Java's swollen, disease-infested main city, Batavia, became the capital of the heterogeneous castes, races and nations of the Orient, so the peoples of the western hemisphere chose Mexico City as the home of their own temporary seat of government.

I dropped into it out of the sky one clear afternoon, only a day following the welcome news that Stephen Dunraven's versatile mind gave to an unhappy world to make men's hearts glad with reborn hope. A waiting motor car took me from the airplane grounds and brought me, an emissary with glad tidings, to the big capitol building of the American Confederacy, where the supervising triumvirate met me. Ten minutes later I was expounding the happy news, Dunraven's scheme of the jetties. The same day Congress voted and passed a bill (a bill that made the State Treasurer blink his eyes) for the building, upkeep, and manipulation of any number of jetties or sea walls and their accessory plants, to be built in many parts of the world. And the powers-that-be on the other half of the globe gladly cried "Aye" to this vote. Telegrams burnt the wires, while wireless tore the ether with tidings of the happiest of messages. That night Mexico City was a bedlam, a happy madhouse of excited men, women and children who had suddenly realized that all hope need not be abandoned after all.

ON the shores of Gold Coast in the central part of mid-western Africa, where the deep and wide Equatorial Current gathers much of its tropical waters destined for more northern zones, the first of the jetties was started, an offspring of the mind of a once rich man who had given up the tinsel parts of life for the more solid ones of science.

I left Vera Cruz, an over-swollen port city on the first workboat to go toward Africa, an erstwhile leviathan ocean greyhound, the Mauretania, formerly of the Cunard Line. Today it was the unquestioned property of the people of the world. It takes mighty cataclysms to do big deeds, and even in the making and unmaking of civilization and of worlds, every dark cloud has its silver lining.

Three weeks went by on shipboard. The Mauretania was a heavy-laden and over-crowded vessel, though on it the hopes of a world rested. It was bearing to the battle front to open up the war—the vanguard of the army that was to combat the glacier.

It was on board the big steamer that I made the acquaint of Major Reginal Cummins, U.S.A., a fatal acquaintance, indeed, to me. The major was a robust man, tall and straight, hitting on the decline side of life. Long years in the uniform had given him a ramrod back that was as straight as any pine that grew in the woods, and though a heavy man with the physique of a heavyweight prize-fighter, he carried his two hundred some odd pounds as a slender Indian carries his hundred and fifty. An energetic egoist of a man, full of the vitality of animal magnetism, brown-eyed, eager, prematurely bald, forever grinning a grin that exposed an even row of very large buck teeth, he reminded me of portraits I had seen of ex-President Roosevelt. Not exactly the man that one would choose to lead, neither was he a man to put at the tail end of the ranks. The clique of nations that made up the American Confederacy had seen fit to send him as a representative to the forefront of the fight. I went along, partly in the capacity of newspaperman, and partly as viceroy of the father of the scheme. We soon struck up an acquaintanceship. It was difficult to strike up a friendship with so vain a man.

CAME the day when the pile-drivers sank the first pillar into the ooze and sand four hundred and eighty feet beneath the choppy, icy surface of the sea. How the finny denizens of the deep must have wondered at this newest intrusion of their ancient pelagic homes. Working men inside of huge metal rooms, veritable ten-men capacity diving bells, were dropped below the waves and from the safety of these undersea workshops started the concrete foundations of this colossal undertaking, the building of the jetty. Upwards and out of the sea rose the huge skeleton frameworks of steel on their bases of stone, the skeletal parts of the gigantic sea wall that was to turn the current and save the world. For two months, one hundred thousand pairs of hands toiled day and night in eight-hour shifts, and one day a line of tall, straight towers of steel rose to an average of five hundred feet skyward, out of the oozy bottom of the sea. At intervals of fifty yards they were for over one hundred miles on the ocean's floor, sometimes only fifty feet beneath the crest of the waves and sometimes one thousand. Later on these towers would be connected with huge girders and these with stanchions, erecting the skeleton framework of the wall of solid concrete and reinforced by steel, one of the armies hurled against the icy foe.

Dunraven came to view his brain-child when it was but half grown, merely a long line of steel towers jutting for fifty feet out of the blue-green sea, and on and about them clustered men, vessels big and little, and man-made islets that housed the workers and their tools. He brought Clara along with him, a jubilant, girlish Clara, who never minded my frayed overalls and enjoyed my bewhiskered company in this anchored city that was fighting desperately to recover from the ice what it had stolen from the world.

That night it stormed with all the fury of an ocean tempest, yet there were four of us who sat, unmindful of it, at the rickety table in my cabin: Stephen Dunraven, his daughter Clara, Major Cummins, and myself, a proud host, over a supper of fish, bread, oleomargarine, and tea. The major was jubilant and the corpulent amateur paleontologist only mirrored him. "It will work, I'm sure," they kept repeating, as if encouraging hopes that sought to stray. Supper over, came cigars, the ubiquitous Ido, as taciturn as ever, superintending their distribution.

"I've tried a little invention of my own," said the man upon whose scheme we were working. "We can superheat with powerful coils the waters of rivers that have their mouths at the regions inundated by the glacier. I endeavored to aid the battle of the jetties with a land skirmish of my own. Thus far I have met with only the most trivial of successes. The heating, of course, was done only on a small scale, a mere experiment, but even then, even a tyro could have foretold that the heat would be dissipated by the cold atmosphere long before it reached the ice, as there was no warmer equatorial current to set it off.

At this point Ido entered with a marconigram and broke up our party. Stephen Dunraven read the message, said a few words to the grinning major concerning some shiploads of concrete, and then they left together. At the door he turned and remarked casually, "It was twenty-two below in Buenos Aires yesterday, while Rio de Janeiro, right under the equator, has hit the zero mark. Never mind the dishes, Clara, Ido will take care of them." A moment later Clara and I were alone.

ADVERSITY gives one courage and hard times make even the weakling bold. I had experienced adversity often in the last twelve months.

"Let's get married, Clara," I said, in an assumed matter-of-fact tone, as soon as the final echo of the feet of the two men on the loose planks had died away into the distance. I knew that my anxious mien belied my assumed tone. But I enjoyed my own audacity.

She did not redden. Girls like Clara never do. Besides that, the last twelve months had left a mark on her, too.

"On what?" she answered me with a question of her own and in the same tone of voice that she would have used had I asked her the time of day; only a tinge of elusiveness colored that tone and betrayed a more than casual feeling.

"On the ice." I was trying to swerve it into a comical channel. And then more seriously, "The same on which you'd marry Paul."

"Oh Paul, fiddlesticks." A pause. "I joined the Red Cross last month, Frank. That is, for active service. Ambulance driving."

"You do like Paul?"

"Well?"

"Do you?"

"Why?"

"Oh, just so. But do you?"

"I've no reason to hate him. Nor you either."

"Good little girl."

"Thanks for the pretty compliment."

"How long do you expect to stay here?"

"Until the jetty is built?" I answered my own question.

"I don't know. Father is anxious to return to his ruins in Mexico. He says that he has evidences of other civilizations even before the spider people. Paul is looking after it now—in a way. He and that little German professor, Herr...oh...Herr whatever his name is."

"Oh pshaw. Let Paul and little Herr German professor look after the spider ruins. Why should your father waste his time there? We, the world, need him much more here. I'd like to see him stay, even if—"

"And me, too?" She spoke softly and tittered, but never looked up from her shoes.

"Yes, of course, you too."

A silence followed. Neither one of us knew what to say, for I dared no longer speak the words I thought. Ido entered with a huge dishpan in one hand and a tiny mop in the other, a miniature article on the model of the kind that housewives use upon their floors. Came the sound of tin ware and of porcelain, and of running water. Clara was humming "Love's Old Sweet Song" softly to herself. I contemplated the frayed toes of my boots for a long while, but said nothing.

Stephen Dunraven, much to my delight, continued to linger on. Major Cummins, more to my delight, became his constant companion. Clara and I saw more and more of each other as the days slipped by and as day by day the long jetty grew out of the sea's bosom, a silent, stationary monster of masonry and steel, a monster which wind and wave buffeted, but which never would give way.

The deluge of ice had stopped, it had found its battle-line, dug-in, as the soldier has it, and though it could advance no farther, it would never relinquish an inch. All over the world on the three big oceans, north and south, the nations were bending their backs over gigantic, sea walls of metal and stone set on the briny's oozy bottom to send pole-ward the warm currents of water to meet the ice. Fang and claw, the world was fighting the ice and fighting hard.

On the opposite side of the globe, the Japs and the Chinese were bending under the burden of a series of jetties that were to send the warmer water of the Equatorial Pacific scurrying into the regions of ice and snow.

In the Bay of Biscay, Europeans labored like madmen to swerve the warm current farther toward the north.

On the coast of Florida, not far from Jacksonville, a small jetty pushed inland the northbound waters of the wide Gulf Stream, that blue river in the green of the ocean.

Jetties everywhere rose out of the depths of the sea as if by magic. Today the waves fell in unbroken, in huge crests, capped with white and in deep hollow troughs, over an even sea, tomorrow a long, level line of steel towers were to lift their skeleton heads skyward out of it, taller than the tallest of its waves. A while later came a wall, a huge edifice of concrete, for an Aladdin's lamp had been rubbed and a world was working overtime.

Nine months earlier the first diving bell descended with its crew and sent word back that they had touched the bottom of the sea, and the concrete foundation of the first pillar of steel was laid then, four hundred and eighty feet below the lowest valley of the waves. The current was turning and the warmer waters were flowing north to meet the ice and end the glacier's marauding career.

IT was one-half a year since the wall had been completed, the first of the lot: and already the big icebergs were tearing themselves away from the main body and drifting southwards with the cold current that came from the Arctic Circle under the surface of the ocean. In reality the Gulf Stream is a trio of warm water streams, about one hundred and seventy-five miles wide with about fifty miles of cold water ribbons between the three warm streams. But now, thanks to the electric superheaters that received their power via wireless from the huge dynamos at Victoria Falls and the manufactured hot carbon-dioxide that warmed the air above them, they became one wide stream of heated water, and flowed with a daily speed of five miles along the American Atlantic coast and then off toward the northeast. And as the glacier melted and receded, smaller jetties, some of them mere anchored sea walls, were swiftly erected at various advantageous points and each jetty comprised a series of huge heating coils that kept warm the southern waters and here and there artificially generated winds kept them going on.

About forty miles of cold water separated the Gulf Stream from the American coast and this "Cold Wall" was pushed rudely aside by a number of smaller sea walls anchored to the ocean's floor. This brought the warmer waters so much nearer to the shore. Later, as the ice gradually melted and as it lessened along our coast, more and more of these "push-over" jetties were put up, until just off Sandy Hook coast where the great warm water stream-current turns northeast and toward the coast of the European nations, a huger jetty was built to prevent the cold under water flow of the Arctic Current from undoing the work of the warm Gulf Stream. Then, after the glacier had been conquered, and the resulting floods allowed it, man vanquished the ice still left on the high hinterlands. Then man could start to rebuild his lost civilization on a land bereft of everything.

So, day by day the huge ice wall retreated and, as it did so, it sent down from its torn breast huge mountains of ice, multi-peaked, brilliant cathedrals, resplendent in the sun, tall, silent sentinels upholding the azure of the sky, the relics and fading monuments of our former destroyer and conqueror.

One morning I arose early and peeked out of the window, where Aurora, on the rippling horizon of the east, had already made pink the skyline that had been as ebony all through the night, and merging sea and sky into one, had built a shimmering pathway of silver on the crest of the waves. A year had elapsed since the first jetty had faithfully answered the hopes and prayers of a waiting world. Now three hundred jetties, big and small, lifted huge concrete backs out of the deep. It was only last night that a swift French destroyer had landed me on the newest one of these, on the Jersey coast, and only a league away from the high ice wall where the song of victory was sung by the warm current as the death-knell of the Sixth Glacier rang through the air. A hundred fathoms deep the warm Gulf Stream was flowing and nearly two hundred miles wide, and it proved a terrible and unrelenting nemesis to the ice that had held us for so long and weary a time.

From Hawaii, now the main center of Japan, news came that a certain army chemist named Bendo had invented a microscopic heat element which, when put into the sea, transformed the current as it traveled with it into an inter-oceanic river of steam. Thin wires of silver in sets of twos were let down to the depth of about five hundred feet and on the end of each was suspended a perforated metal plate, thick with a gluey solution, which in time threw off the hot electronic particles, which flowed in a steady stream with the current and keeping their heat for many miles, made a seething cauldron out of the current-streams of the deep.

It was this that had from the very beginning proved so dire a foe to the ice kings from the poles. I watched them often as they sent the superheated Gulf Stream, seething and foaming, deep into the heart of the ice fields and spreading an invisible blanket of warmth over the land for five hundred miles inwards from the coast.

Electric heaters, we quite properly named them and we found them to be very, effective also in combating the ice-infested rivers, which flowed toward the poles. As they melted the mile thickness of ice that lay over the streams and sent floods everywhere, they left a bright chasm a mile deep and many miles wide, as the newest river bed, with tall walls of ice rising on either side.

CHAPTER TWELVE
An So At Last the Ice Gave Way

AND then came the floods. Oceans of water were let loose. The unfortunate ones near rivers and shores were trapped like rats in a swollen sewer. Higher and higher rose the seas, wherever bays were narrow or coasts were low; at times they even covered the tops of jetties. And as they went southwards, they inundated many beaches and often left behind them huge hills of ice.

And not only did those lands which were nearest to the melting wall of ice feel the damage of the flood; those which bordered the swollen rivers also were affected. Beaten and kicking its last, the Sixth Glacier struck out at those whom it failed to get before.

Italy was using volcanic heat, and huge jets or streams of hot water were uncovering lost lands on that boot-shaped peninsula. A one-time fortunate eruption of Vesuvius threw up large quantities of hot gases and cut a large patch out of the ice field that covered Naples. The Mediterranean Sea was still one huge cake of ice for the warmth of the current could not pass the strait of Gibraltar.

HAPPY was the world of fugitives who lived in the torrid zone, gradually coming into its own again. Slowly the big walls of ice retreated northward and southward, here a jagged piece fell into the sea, there an overhanging mass dropped with a monstrous splash and was carried toward the equator on the crest of the waves. And then one day, when the warm air and water spread and cut grooves into the ice range, entire miles fell into the sea as if by the stroke of a magician's wand. Newer cities were daily planned and newer lands were divided among those who had lost everything when the ice came from the poles. Even now, braving the terrors of the coastal floods, families were dropping into the relinquished lands, slowly to be sure, but pioneers would never be pioneers if they came in hordes or in vast multitudes.

Famished nomads roamed the bleak interiors of the ice-fields where cities and towns once had stood, and where millions once upon a time had lived, toiled, played, loved and died. There these desperate creatures, from whom hunger and cold had taken the final vestiges of civilization, eked out a cruel existence by hunting, trapping, fishing, and robbing one another, and whenever these methods failed, a ghastly cannibalism took their place. Of course, many of these people eventually found themselves in some outlying igloo village set on the fringe of the halted glacier where the first of the pioneers were awaiting the bugle-call to advance. Others however merely wandered to and fro on the crest of the glacier or finding a temporary nook safe froth wind and hunger, erected homes of snow.

The broad prairies of the Argentine, the Chilean, Mexican, and North African desert sand-wastes, the Veldts of South Africa's spared regions, the mountainous countries of the Andes, Cordilleras, Sierra Madre, with the fertile vales, and the swampy regions of the tropical lowlands, together with the South Seas and parts of Asia, were the havens of refuge of ten millions. The peoples of every tongue and clime started life anew there, on almost nothing, and fought as only the desperate can fight for their existence.

And then one day the sun came out. Reports from several newer astronomical observatories (reconstructed from the salvaged material of the older ones), had it that safety and rescue were in view and that the outer fringes of the vast inter-spacial belt of cold was not far off. And so at last the ice gave way.

FOUR weeks went by and with them went the end of the frigid belt. Hundreds of gigantic icebergs menaced the ships that were already carrying northward those, who had only three years ago fled in panic before the ice, and also the tiny newcomers who had never experienced the ordeal of those dreadful days.

And as the ice melted, the floods came and a second deluge threatened the world, its menace as terrible as that of the icy flood that had preceded it. Rivers became roaring cataracts that defied everything. And with the torrents came huge cakes of ice that jammed at narrows and formed silvery dikes. The mad waters flooded the countryside for miles around. Airplane bombs blew these ice walls into glittering, oriental smithereens, which became rainbows, as the powerful ex-plosive hurled them high into the air. Then sidetracked waters receded back into their original tormented beds. The land was full of lakelets, wherever there was hollow ground.

The Mississippi, torn from its pre-glacial channels by three years of moving ice, proved to be a terrible Father of Waters, New Orleans became a ghastly, death-trap to almost three million people early in the season of the big thaw. One night the inhabitants were told that there was no danger and then, as the town clocks chimed out the death knell of another day, that most dreadful of cries wrung the sleepers ears: "Awake, awake. The waters are rising." The sun of the next morning looked sadly down upon a demolished city and its three million dead, one vast graveyard that fifty feet of flood water claimed as its own.

Wide, shallow torrents crisscrossed the deserts of the southwest for the sands offered but the poorest of river beds. Los Angeles was flooded and San Pedro, twenty miles away and by the sea, was just swept away. Sacramento became a veritable Venice as the river, that coursed by it, rose. The remnants of San Francisco, which the glacier had spared, were all swept away into the sea. The Colorado River became one huge lake covering four states, and where the deep gorge of the Grand Canyon impeded its way; it became a raging, tearing fury of brown, foamed with milky white, a demon of water. The Rio Grande too, became a lake and on its bottom was El Paso with only the hills of Fort Bliss above the muddy water.

From where Seattle once stood, southeastward on a more or less, irregular line, to the place where Salt Lake City once was, thence on a straight course to the north rim of the Grand Canyon, eastward from there in a snaky line to the snow-capped Rockies, skirting, their sides only to orient itself toward the Great Lakes and thence out to the Atlantic, was the newest line of battle of the Sixth Glacier.

Europe and Asia was still covered north of the Alps and the Balkans, over the Black Sea where it formed a low, irregular wall, and thence defied the sun on the north side of the Himalayas. Australia and Africa were entirely free, though Capetown, Sydney and Melbourne were no more. Tierra del Fuego was still in the glacier's grip.

Somewhere a bit north of Denver, a city one mile above the level of the sea and framed by many mountain peaks, was to be our new national capital, and though yet fast in the glacier's grasp, the plans were made and the men were ready.

New river courses found homes in the late desert lands, and the fertile soil, washed down from hill and stolen from Arctic vale, sent us sagebrush and Manzanita, threefold as much as of yore. On the banks of rivers, tules and arrow-weeds sprang up as if by magic, and all indications pointed, toward verdant fields, where once only scrub-brush grew.

A score of cities with their outlying farm districts grew like mushrooms overnight, not huge cities of towers and minarets, but long, straight avenues that stretched across the flat lands or ran up and down the hills, treeless and barren, homes of canvas, of mud and of stone. Lands were tilled and crops sown and people lived anew on the northland's finest of soils, brought down by the glacier as the war indemnity of a conquered foe.

Came Thanksgiving Day, the last Thursday in November of that happy year and the whole world made it a day of joy. Although but one day was proclaimed, that day grew into one whole week.

It was at about this time that the Pan-American Federation of Nations broke up, broke up in bad blood with one group demanding millions as rental debts, and another group, just as impoverished, moving out and refusing to pay. War for a while seemed imminent, but as there were no spoils for the victors, the newest of war-clouds drifted away amidst grumbling and curses. In such catastrophes, the lands of the earth are the possessions of no particular ones, but of all who seek shelter there.

Greece was the first of Europe to be freed. Italy came next, then Spain and France, together with the lower Balkans. Turkey had never been in the real grip of the glacier, and though it had suffered many boreal days and months, the land of the crescent and the scimitar never felt the icy grip from the pole that its neighbors had. Persia was first cleared in Asia, and, in our own country, Maryland was the first state to free itself of the Sixth Glacier.

THEN one day war broke out in Brazil. A group of huge national "ghettoes" had sprung up automatically with the influx of North Americans and Europeans. Lands were cleared and farms and houses were erected. Hamlets became towns and sometimes, cities, too much of hard labor's offsprings to expect men to give up without a struggle. And yet the new, fate-driven settlers not only refused to become citizens of the settled lands, they refused to leave even when the glacier retreated from their erstwhile homes. In fact they became distant colonists of a barren motherland. Days of bloodshed followed, skirmishes, massacres, battles, while carcasses rotting beneath the tropical sky fed the birds of the air, and smoldering ash heaps held reign, where only a while ago towns had been. Finally disease became the grand conqueror and germs proved more terrible weapons than bayonets and bullets, and a train of sick and weary armies marched home, unhaloed and unsung.

Of course many died in this grand exodus from a refugee's home, but also many a one was born on that northward march. It was not like the mad stampede of three years ago, when a panic-stricken multitude trampled the weak and left the sick behind. The returning armies came in more orderly fashion. Group by group, with tearful parting which smiles belied, as one throng received its orders to start, singing poems of victory, they marched home, defying the floods.

CHAPTER THIRTEEN
The People of the Glacier

ONE day while at the new settlement of Dunravenia, on the scarlet south rim of the Grand Canyon, the flap of my little tent was thrown rudely to one side, and Clara ushered herself in with a whirl of snow. Close behind her, and grinning like a huge Cheshire cat, was the big boyish Major Cummins, U. S.

A. Little was said on any side. Clara was in a hurry to go to the aid of some storm-stricken igloo villages in northern Utah,—the big major knew of nothing to say; as for me—my heart was too full for me to give vent to my thoughts, so we bowed to one another and bid good-byes, promising to meet again on some summer day. Clara left a letter behind her and even before I cut the flap of the envelope, I recognized the almost effeminate hand of the portly amateur of science, whose timely warning had saved so many lives. Clara gave my hand a petulant squeeze, which I wished could linger on, and she promised to call again as soon as her Red Cross duties would allow. Paul, she told me, had only recently arrived, and then she lost herself in the narrow confines of a rather diminutive aero-sedan, and even as she locked the door behind her, my quick eyes caught the sight of a glittering diamond on her left hand, which, I knew well, had not been there for very long. "Paul," I said to myself, half aloud, "you've won. Congratulations old man and happy days. But how in the world did you do it?" The age-old lament of the beaten lover. Then a moment later I reflected: "What is she gallivanting around with the old major for?" I asked myself, and echo answered, feebly though, "Oh, yes; he, too, is going north to succor the hungry and frozen ice dwellers. He's an army man." However, I slept poorly that night.

Paul came to see me at noon the next day, a woebegone Paul, downcast and haggard. To my halfhearted congratulations, he turned an askance, mien. "Bosh," was his momentary expression and a sickly smile crossed his face. Then he continued in a chilling "What-do-I-care" tone of voice. Not me, old boy," he said slowly. "I'm in the same boat with you. Congratulate the right one," Though gone was my love, I slept a trifle sounder that night. Misery does love company.

For two days, Dunraven's missive had gone unread. My mind was too full for scientific gossip. Strangely, the tie which, a short while ago had held me so firmly to the elder man, was now somehow no more. His scientific rantings appeared no longer to hold an interest for me, and I found my idol to be of clay. "Bah," I ejaculated peevishly as I sat partly dressed on the edge of my cot. "What do I care about him and his?"

However, I read the letter, though hastily. Dunraven predicted a world of involuntary vegetarians, and later years proved this to be too true. The spider people of his discovery had made use of poisoned arrows, some of the arrow-points having been found. The aged German savant had broken his foot, while attempting to carry a part of a very ancient cannon out of a very deep excavation. A handle-less stone battle-ax, more likely than not of an Eolithic era, was also unearthed by the sleepless bloodhounds of science, reminiscent of the by-gone glories of the ape-man's days; it told how he fought the spider race which conquered and enslaved him with poisoned dart and iron shot. "That these so very interesting creatures were fairly on their way to bid toward a kind of humanity is more or less ascertained by the noticeable absence of any silk-sacs on the pictures of themselves which they had left behind them before relentless time claimed them, their last pictures that are growing in number with each stroke of the pick," the letter went on to say in part. Then followed a very natural lament against the lack of any scientific spirit in the new Mexican government which was even now casting an evil eye on the little Yankee city that had risen around the ruins. The letter ended up with a long tirade on the speculation of the government and the social system of the spiders, about their mode of home life, and whether they laid eggs or belonged to some extinct order of ethnological mammalia. Of Clara, nothing.

I sighed a very audible "aw," and threw the letter into a corner of the tent. The following day I made ready for a trip to Tampa.

Those rivers which flowed toward the pole were harnessed by the returning home-seekers to carry into the heart of the frozen lands the great electrical heat waves that melted the ice, and as these worked only in salt water, an almost endless procession of salt trains came from all directions of the compass on the newly constructed narrow-gauge railways or by huge trucks over the roads.

So rapid is the healthy recovery of Nature, that in no more than one year's time, the tropics became the tropics again and though palm and banyan did not flourish until later, the natives were already beginning to forget those cold days which carried them off, and thick undergrowth came up almost overnight. Hearth and home of noisy insect life were resumed and there were huge ferns; such as paleobotanical treatises allow to the Carbonaceous Era, in the days when most of our coal was made. They were as tall as trees and as lithe as tules. And as the ice-driven white settlers returned to their northern homes, they left behind to the dark-hued, thick-lipped natives tilled acres and hastily built villages, relics of civilization, as payment for the three years of safety there. Just another chapter in the unwritten annals of civilization, mankind's slow conquest of Nature in her fiercest of moods—mute, ceaseless struggles. All unrecorded.

Brown, gray, and mauve hills, their broad backs once covered with forests, now carried tiny left-over glaciers, and their fertile valleys, opulent with three years of accumulation of northern soil, were covered with many feet of snow. For a long time the lowlands were soggy, while the river valleys were constantly at the mercy of newer and newer floods. Where gigantic cities once upon a time, had stood, now to be located only by latitude and longitude, there were but flat terrains or low, rolling lands, arid, lifeless, barren—mute witnesses to show where the polar ice had crushed all as it passed in its might. Yet if one dug in places deep enough, some bit of iron or stone would appear as a reward, a relic out of more orderly times, which the glacier had failed to carry off.

There was no wood, for the reclaimed world was treeless, and families had to start life all over again in houses of mud and stone or in tents of canvas. Long, straight avenues, bordered on each side by wind-flapped tents or by sturdy adobe walls, overlooked naked plains or hilly countries that rose and fell away toward the horizon. Surrounding them were patches of green that seemed to bow before each breeze, where the first buds of the newly sown gifts of the soil had only a few days ago left their dark underground homes to take their first peep at the blue of the sky.

THOSE people who had braved the ice, and defying boreal days, had played Eskimo on the glacier's back, were glad to see the end of their game, and their igloo homes destroyed by the sun as the ice gave way. Like savages they either roamed the unbounded ice fields or hid in the precarious safety of their little snow-houses, emerging only when hunger became the incentive. There on the glacier's back they formed the desperate vandal bands that knew no law but that of self-preservation, or became the quieter igloo-villagers who hunted the polar bear and the Arctic fox in order to exist.

Four years had already gone by since the first panic-stricken refugee started for the south, and by this time the ice had already receded until only the lands north of the Canadian border were still in the glacier's grasp. There were still irregular patches of ice here and there, long arms of the mightiest of glaciers that projected forth into the higher regions of the continent as if the polar foe were reluctant to give back to man the land that was his own. In the mountainous districts of Colorado, Idaho, Wyoming, and Montana, the Sixth Glacier still stretched long icy arms and there remnants of the polar demon still remained to tell of those terrible days when pandemonium broke loose and reigned over the world. North of that all was still the glacier's own. A squadron consisting of seven motor-sleds and their huge lorries, all of them overloaded with provisions, went to succor a group of survivors who for four years had eked out a slim livelihood in the high mountain regions of the Yellowstone. In the vicinity of the Teton Basin, this government train was overtaken and looted by a gypsy band of famished snow-dwellers, men and women, whom four years of hardship and deprivations had returned to the cave ages. Upon report of this newest outrage, one of the many of its kind, the government immediately dispatched a small fleet of fast, heavily armed motor-sleds, accompanied by an escadrille of flying machinery, to break up the boreal banditry that, like the attacks of the red skins of old, came down in silence and stealth on the northernmost outpost settlements. Even at his best, man is but a short three hundred generations removed from the caves and a hirsute, large-tusked forbear's ghost is with us yet, and an empty stomach understands no rules and regulations.

There was a battle during a snow-storm, the strangest battle in history. Huge balls of snow, that became huger with each turn, came down from the hill-tops and buried part of our train in an avalanche. Machine guns, tear-bombs, rifles, grenades, and aerial missiles, however, soon routed the looters from their snowy fastnesses. Like covered beasts, they fought the fur-clad soldiers in ravines, on slippery mountain-tops, and the prisoners that the soldiers could take were few. As a representative of a journal which was the first to decry the coming terror, I was allowed to interview them—emaciated men and women of another eon—and in scattered phrases learned the story of four years of terrible life on the glacier's back.

They were landed a day later in a temporary camp, still a bit scared and wild. Busy with my camera, I failed to notice the arrival of half a dozen Red Cross sleds and they left before I was able to see Clara, who was among the Red Cross workers.

A day passed, a day spent in motor-sledding back to the site of the proposed new national capital, Washingtonia, I directed my footsteps to the gigantic wood and corrugated-tin edifice which housed the multitude of wards of the emergency hospital. A pompous, middle-aged chief orderly with the imperturbable air of a floorwalker, let me know in a brief sentence, that neither Clara nor the contingent of Red Cross sleds to which she belonged, had as yet arrived. Then leaving me rooted to the bare wooden floor of the building, he returned and strode majestically down the long corridor, his heavy footsteps echoing throughout the spacious place. Later one of the night nurses let me know that although they were expecting the arrival of the other Red Cross sleds at any moment, not a few fears were felt for the safety of the few men and women who made up the personnel of the train of sleds. A wireless message from the military sled outfit with which I had been and which even now was scouring the snow covered hills and valleys for any sign of the predatory rovers on the glacier's back, had given warning to all of the outlying newly formed settlements to be on their guard, as hostile bands of crazed, hunger-stricken men and women, those whom four long years of deprivation after deprivation had hurled back into the antediluvian eons and the days of the caves, were outraging the countryside with looting and murder. That night I slept little.

EARLY the next morning, the rising sun still below the crimson of the eastern skyline, Major Cummins, only partly dressed and very unmilitary-like in his four days' growth of bristling beard, broke wildly into my tent and between pantings of breath, and accompanied by maniacal gesticulations, each of which threatened my clothing, strung out on a line between the tent poles, told me in excited words, that Clara had been kidnapped by a horde of hungry igloo-villagers who considered themselves neglected by the food distributing committees. She was now being held for ransom to appease gnawing stomachs. Their terms were arbitrary and the alternative too gruesome to relate. Fifteen minutes later we were speeding northward as fast as a propeller-driven motor-sled could take us. At noon we were searching the remains of what once had been a Red Cross train of sleds. Night found us in the lower regions of the mountainous Teton Basin, south of Yellowstone National Park, still well within the chilly grasp of the Sixth Glacier. Only the snow-laden tops of the many tall peaks protruded above the world of ice, which seemed to encompass all, as far as the eye was able to see. The next morning we were prisoners in the hands of the starved villagers, who had seen us arrive and had awaited only darkness and the night to pounce upon us.

That an unappeased hunger had brought cannibalism upon these unfortunate people, the many human bones scattered about their snow dwellings told only too well. I pointed this out to the army man, who immediately turned pale beneath his stubby growth of beard. "We must make terms with them— any terms they like," was all that he could find to say. And then a couple of minutes later, "My God. My God!" I turned my head and looked at him. His huge head was lost in his pair of huge fur-gloved hands. "Cannibals," he was saying to himself, as if there were no one close enough to hear, "and we've only been married eleven days." A moment later he turned to me, anxiety in both of his wide-opened eyes. "But they're after good food just now and not human flesh. Isn't it so, Bender? They'll never eat her. No, never. She's only a hostage to make sure that we bring the grub. We'll treat them right by all means and promise to send up the chow-wagons right away and they'll surely let her go. Don't you think so? Sure." My answer was almost an inarticulate "Uh-huh," nearly a grunt, for my chin had fallen and I felt like a beaten dog. Relegated to the lowest limboes was my final shred of hope, and just like any other beaten, love-sick swain, I was a silent, morose man. "The army had won again," was the sole half-audible remark I made after a half-hour of wicked thoughts, before I coiled up on my wolf-skin bed on the snow. A moment later I was in a dreamless slumber.

Next day at noon, inside of his igloo, we stood face to face with the chieftain of the hungry tribe, a very big and hirsute man, wrapped in furs. It was not difficult to surmise that sheer strength and brutality had given him a footing on the clan's loftiest pedestal and had kept him there and even now allowed him to hold unqualified sway. Four young, thin faced women hovered sycophantly about him, a quartette of fur-clad butterflies. Three be-whiskered men, armed with rifles, stood menacingly behind us. The hungry clan leader eyed me as the famished wolf would eye the well-fed dog. Then for a brief instant his eyes rested on the Major's fur coat. "An army man, eh," he commented with a leer that exposed a very irregular row of teeth. "Well, old boy, we'll army you here, all right."

For our words of succor and food from the government, the burly men had complete contempt. The fact of the general helplessness, in the face of the glacier and the vast magnitude of the ice fields, never seemed to have entered his mind. He talked as a peevish child might talk, who had thought himself unjustly wronged. He never appeared to grasp the world-wideness of the situation and answered only in an egocentric way.

"If the government is so bent upon feeding us, then why didn't it feed us all along? We were here for four years, hungry all the time. One by one we starved and died, and then, because there was absolutely nothing else to eat, we ate the dead. Mere skin and bones they were, but we ate them. My wife and my four kiddies died the first year, one after the other, but what was that to the big ones safe in the White House down in Washington? They had plenty to eat, I'm sure. You talk about the Red Cross. Well, no Red Cross came here in four long years. They just allowed us to go hungry. And then you wonder why we steal. Anybody will steal when he's hungry."

My arguments and explanations, or rather my hasty and puny efforts at such, were futile, for the man was unable to grasp the vastness of the catastrophe and the world's helplessness before it. It never entered his mind that the very government which he thought had neglected him so direfully, had been non-existent during all of the four years during which he went hungry. I endeavored to show him the wrong impressions that he labored under, but as every word of mine tended to enrage him, I realized the value of the ancient adage that silence is golden.

WHEN we returned to our fur-floored prison of snow, the major became voluble again. He feared the teeth of these cannibal snow-dwellers for his young bride; he feared the harem of the burly leader more. I allowed him to talk on for about an hour or so when in the steady outpour of his Niagara of words he made his one rational, although unconscious, remark:

"I really do believe, Bender," he said, "that—that big fellow believes us to be on the square. He really thinks he'll be fed and that we mean rescue, but then there's really something else in the wind back there. Once upon a time, you know, he had nothing; probably he was only a day laborer or a farmer. He's big enough, now, however. He's king. A real honest-to-goodness King and his word is law. He doesn't appear to be starved to me. Did you notice how they all jumped whenever he spoke to them? I did. A return to civilized ways once more would mean to him, the return of the King to the farm and the plow, or to the forge. You know what Caesar answered the Roman Senate when they wanted him to come back to Rome and be second in command: "It's better to play first fiddle in Iberia than second fiddle in bigger Rome." This man seems to think so, too. A life of comparative ease now. Anything obtainable at his command. I'm sure that he never went hungry. And did you see his wives? I wonder if he intends to include Clara in his harem?"

In answer, I smiled an almost demoniacal smile. A blighted lover, even at his best, is but a poor companion; and he is of very much less value when the victor is at his side.

We received no food. I recalled the human bones which I had seen scattered about the camp and my hunger was appeased. The major, however felt otherwise. He cursed them volubly and in no uncertain terms and told me many stories of savages who fed their captives.

"Maybe they wanted to fatten them," I answered grimly, but he merely contemplated me with a peculiar glance and made no remark in return.

Late that evening, we heard a scattered series of shots coming from the direction of the village, shots that the mountains roared back at the sky. Five minutes passed riotously, then the tumult and shouting died away. A minute later our three armed guards fired twice apiece and then were lost beneath a pile of waving arms and legs. A couple of fur-clad bodies hugging closely the snow that was even then swiftly becoming dyed a gruesome scarlet, showed where two of the guardsmen's bullets had hit their mark. Shouts of "home again" and of "let's go back" reached our ears from the main part of the igloo settlement. A sudden revolt, pent up by many cruel days, had burst forth, and the big, fur-clad King was dead, his Kingdom gone arid his adhering sycophants scattered to the winds. Too many lean days had driven these men and women, who had known better times, to desperation and a desire to return to the civilized life that was awaiting them. There was no King to stand in their way now.

Little use it was to give them any assurance of safety. These people had known terrible times. Most of them even doubted that the fight was finally won, that the glacier was even now retreating. "It's still snowing, is it not?" they would say and regard us with the disdain with which one regards a prevaricator. "Even if the glacier has stopped due to your jetties, it stopped only in the tropics and on the shore-lands. Here we are too far from the coast and too high up in the air for warm sea currents to do us any good. And then too, these winters are so long, so very long—and so very cold. Panama is too far a distance for us, half-starved as we are, to travel over a world of ice. Locked in by these few salvaged mountain peaks we are to some extent safe, even if we are hungry and we do not care to risk the furies, of the Arctic gales on the lower plain lands below. If the heads of this new government that you talk about really do want to help us and are our friends, then why do they not send us food and fuel instead of armored sleds and soldiers with guns? Isn't Nature cruel enough with her ice and storms?

"However, if you two are sincere and are really speaking the truth, then go home, let them know how we stand here and return with pardons and with food. We'll find some way out after that. But no soldiers, for remember this…" (and here a score of hard, sunken eyes gleamed upon the major) "…we've got the girl. She is our hostage and the ransom is food."

A newcomer entered the group, a cadaverous youth, hollow-eyed and prematurely aged. In his hands he carried some bits of broiled meat, almost black from too much oven fire. He handed it to me, reluctantly, as if giving up part of himself.

"For your trip," he said. "They'll give you some guns too. Don't be afraid to eat it, buddy. It ain't human flesh. It's coyotes' paws. Kind o' burned, but still better'n nothin' at all. An' say, hurry back with some real grub, will you?"

"Well, here's one at least that has a bit of faith in us," I told the silent major. My judgment, however, was short-lived, for scarcely had we gone a hundred steps when the thin youth shouted after us. "Hey, you guys," came his high pitched nasal tone, and there was not a little malice coupled with it. "Better bring the grub, else we'll eat that girl." The major's legs became springs that instant. "Let's hurry," he said, "and bring them something to eat. The poor devils are starving."

We found our motor-sled almost intact where the hungry igloo-dwellers had left it on the night of their stealthy attack. Only the wooden parts of it were gone, for the nights were very cold here and fuel was at a premium. I started the motor and it purred hopefully.

Then followed a quarter hour or so of silence. The military man was drumming on the glass of the useless and shaky door, which rattled with each vibration of the speeding sled. Once we passed a sample of heavily fur-clad men on long and awkward snow-shoes with rifles in their mittened hands. They walked laboriously, as if the journey had been long and tedious and the snow had been deep. One had a dead fox slung over his shoulder.

We were now entering a slope made hazardous to such travel by a series of very sharp curves. Huge pillars of ice jutting out of the snow made speed impossible. I had just put all of my weight on the foot brake mechanism which released a heavy spiked beam into the soft snow under the running sled and at the same instant stopped the huge propeller which pulled the sled forward and had shouted to my companion to take hold of the emergency brake lever at his side, when I felt the icy floor beneath us giving way. At the same time I was aware of a crash that sounded like a million icepicks at work at once. Down we slid on the tumultuous crest of an avalanche, men, machine, lee, snow, rocks, for about a quarter of a mile away from the mountain-top home of the igloo-people that loomed like an island out of the shining flat back of the glacier. A moment passed and we were pushing our way fiercely and ponderously through a huge snowbank. Then everything came to a sudden standstill. We emerged scared, shaken, but uninjured. The wrecked auto-sled lay, a mass of twisted iron of the hill. A long, straight trail, cut in the snow above us, showed the route we had come.

"It's all over now, I guess," I remarked as I contemplated the hopeless wreck. "And it looks like snow. Much snow." The sky was like lead.

"Night will be upon us soon too." Thus from the major.

"Oh well, it always is—sooner or later."

"It's four now by my wrist-watch. Is there no way out? No way to fix 'er?"

I shook my head slowly.

"About how far are we from the nearest settlement?"

"Four hundred miles at a very conservative estimate."

"Four hundred miles—gee! We might try going back. Why not?"

For answer I pointed to the almost perpendicular wall above us.

"Uh. Oh, yes. Guess we can't, at that. No chance for climbing. Isn't there some way to repair the machine, though? We have tools."

"We have them scattered over about a quarter mile of snow. Yes"

"Gosh, but you seem to take it easy. There's lives depending on us, man."

"Well, what do you suggest?"

"Uh. Can't fix 'er, that's certain. Let's see."

He was gone for a few minutes and I could hear him tinkering with the wreck.

"No use," he said upon returning, fur and face marked with black grease spots. "The motor fell out. I got the guns, though. We very likely will need them. Huh—what was that?"

"Sounded like wolves to me."

"Wolves."

"Yes, I guess so. Wolves or coyotes. Better let me have one of those rifles."

A LITTLE while later we were inspecting the wreckage together. Repair was absolutely beyond possibility. In the rapid flight to the base of the hill, the entire fore part of the sled had broken loose and was now buried in deep snow somewhere between the base and the summit. The top and one of the sides were crushed in. The radiator was gone, as was the battery. One of the light aluminum-steel runners was twisted into a spiral as if done by a Cyclopean hand and the light rapid-firer was torn from its tripod. We were lucky men to have escaped alive.

"No, it's no use; absolutely no use," I told the major. "We'll have to stay until something turns up. That is, unless you care to try four-hundred miles of snow, or this hill above us. I don't know which would be worse."

Once more the series of long drawn-out howls arose and pierced the air. This time they seemed nearer.

"The wolves are calling to each other," I said, fingering my rifle nervously. "They have sighted us. Keep close to your gun, Cummins. Let's try to fix that rapid-firer. It may come in handy. Better have some gasoline and matches near at hand. The tank's intact, I hope. Have you a flashlight?"

Night came upon us suddenly and brought with it the wind and snow. It fell in streaks, about as fast as snow could fall. It never fluttered, it fell down in chunks and small masses and covered everything in a few seconds' time with a blanket of smooth whiteness. At intervals of a few minutes, the vandal beasts of the ice fields mad with appetite, continued their weird, ominous calls.

It must have been somewhat past midnight, before the wolf-pack howled itself into enough courage to attack. The grim, gnawing pangs of hunger make even the most cowardly brave, the most discreet reckless, the most lamb-like fierce. The snowfall had abated to some extent, but the thick flakes were still coming down and covering our wrecked sled, amidst the twisted tin and iron, where we had taken refuge from both beast and element. We had decided upon the plan of each taking four hour shifts on guard duty, while the other slept. I was allowed the first shift at sleep, huddled up among a pair of heavy blankets, which the people of the glacier had returned to us, and my own huge fur coat. It seemed only a minute after I had fallen asleep that the major awoke me. In the flare of the burning gasoline, I could see that his eyes were weary, like those of a man who had only now left behind him a long, hard illness. He pointed to a couple of Springfields near at hand.

"They sound nearer every minute," he let me know in a low, sepulchral tone. "Once I was even able to see the gleam of eyes, a score of twinkling, green pinpoints. Dark as all hell outside; and I'm sleepy. Keep pouring gas into that tin-plate or the fire will go out and they'll attack. No snow's falling in.

I fixed our roof, and fearing that the weight would crush it in, I kept the snow brushed off. It's four o'clock now and not so very far away from dawn, so let's hope for the best. There's some cigarettes on the seat next to you. Better light up. A fag is a good companion on a lonely watch. I can testify to that. Good night."

The night was cold and the wind blew hard and wafted to my ears the long drawn-out, eerie yelp of the predatory beasts, made mad by hunger's unrelenting lash. I found the major's cigarettes and took his advice. Then, with nothing better to do, I fingered the magazine of one of the rifles and made the other ready for combat at a moment's notice. The snow kept falling steadily but as the wind came from an opposite direction, it did not bother me. I was safe behind the shelter of the wrecked auto-sled. At times, however, the strong blast from off the plains threatened to push sled and all, over on its side and I began to have apprehensions for our little stronghold. Also, under the weight of the accumulated snow, the weak roof was beginning to give way, protesting as it did so with cracks and groans. So with rifle in one hand and flashlight in the other, I crawled through the battered door of the sled and out into the wind and snow.

I felt as the storm-struck mariner must feel, when he is aroused from his slumbers by the call of the mate at midnight, or when amidst the wild diapason of wave, wind, and human throat, he hears the most dreaded yell of those who dare the seven seas, "All hands on deck to man the life-boats." I lowered my head like an angry bull as I bucked the gale-driven snowflakes. In the near distance the wolves howled and I could see the reflection of my tiny gasoline fire in a hundred green eyes. I fired a wanton shot and for a few minutes there was a silence. Then I heard the major's excited voice.

"What is it, Bender? Ho, Bender, where are you?"

His words ended in a scream and amid the crack of his gun, I could hear the scraping of paws and the sounds of struggle within the sled. I arrived as the light went out, a wolf yelped a cry of pain, and Major Cummins' gun barked out again, a stentorian, staccato noise above the howls of the hungry pack. A long, furry body fell heavily at my feet. I turned my flashlight on the major. The man was a born soldier. In a moment I was at his side.

"Light the fire quick, Bender," he snapped out in a naturally commanding voice, sharp and sudden. "My God, man, what was your idea in leaving. That's all they were waiting for. It's a lucky thing for you that you came back alive. Good, she's lit. Keep 'er like that. Our lives depend on that flare just now. Are you sure that we're safe on all four sides? Better get your light and see. We can't take any risks, you know. But I wish it was daylight. Here they come again. Look at their eyes."

Three score green spots, flickering with evil intent, appeared suddenly in the dark about a hundred feet or so from us. The major had automatically taken command, for it was battle and war was his trade. At his advice, I poured more gasoline into our makeshift burner. He fired three times in rapid succession and a howl of pain rang out in the night. A series of low, hoarse growls contrasted grimly with it as the unfortunate victim of the old soldier's aim was being devoured by his famished fellow hunters.

"We've got to go easy on our ammunition," remarked the major smiling and I began to like him a bit. Now, at his own game, he was very different from the man I knew.

THEN for a long while, it seemed a year, the howling continued. It seemed to harmonize with the voice of the wind. At the price of two broken pocket-knife blades and a cut thumb, I managed to cut some strips of tin. Folding these into a cup-like shape, we filled them with a gasoline, of which the tank happily was still rather full. Thus we had in instant readiness a dozen or more of very crude incendiary bombs in case of a second attack. The major had sallied forth into the darkness and had brought back with him the limp body of the second riddled beast, which fell quite close to the side. It was an Airedale dog, gaunt, shaggy and fierce, with a red hole behind his right ear.

"Wild dogs, not wolves," commented the major in a more or less surprised tone. "Once upon a time man's best friend and companion, now gone back to the savage stage again; just as these igloo-people have gone back to the days of the caves. It caused men to become cannibals; little wonder then that hunger should drive a dog into a wild animal stage again."

"Yes," I interjected, "it's only a few thousand years since this was their regular life. Let's throw him out to the pack; maybe it'll ease their appetites a bit and make them less eager for us."

It was at this moment that the first wild dog jumped into the opened door and threw me bodily to the floor of the sled. I felt a cold snout at my throat and unloosening my glove, got hold of a handful of coarse, fuzzy hair. An icy paw clawed at my face and I heard a rumbling growl only a few inches away in the ebony of the darkness. I kicked the beast loose after an effort and then as I arose, I heard the major's rifle. I picked up my own and fired twice at the open doorway where a dark shadow appeared to merge into the surrounding shadows. I was rewarded by a yelp of pain and then sharp teeth tore at my fur coat and I fell again. I beat at the head of my canine attacker with the barrel of my rifle and then the heavy body of my companion rolled on top of me, panting, fighting silently. Someone was tearing viciously at my right boot and with the other I placed a heavy kick on a head and as the teeth gave way, I heard a yelp of pain. Somewhere during the turmoil I had picked up a big wrench, the sole survivor of a large set of tools, and with this I beat at the furry assailants on the major's back. A rifle is such an unwieldy weapon when the combat is hand to hand. The major fired once more, emitted a horrible oath, and then I heard the pounding of huge fists on cracking ribs. A moment later I was on my feet.

In the flare of our small gasoline burner, ghostly in the whirling snow drift, I saw an eager, waiting pack outside, red tongues licking icy chops. God help us, I thought, if some of these hunger-maddened beasts succeed in dragging us out from behind the comparative safety of our little fort. With that I lit one of our improvised gasoline bombs and hurled it into the midst of the yelping pack of dogs. For a moment they stood their ground nobly—only for a moment. Four years of savage life had completely reverted them into the primitive wolf-pack ages; it made them fear fire, and the pack gave way as if struck by a thousand furies. The major was still struggling and once or twice I heard him curse. The next moment found me at his side. I kicked, I struck, I tore, I fired my rifle and hurled my grenades. The gasoline burner suddenly went out as a huge body fell against it. A dog yelped loudly in agony and jumped through the doorway and disappeared into the night and the snow-drift, his side smoldering with the burning gasoline. I heard the stock of the Major's Springfield fall heavily upon something that cracked sharply beneath it, once, twice and then three times and the next moment we were alone again.

"Quick, Bender," the major was speaking in an even, unperturbed tone. "Light that gas again, or they'll be back upon us. Damn 'em for a thousand furies. I'm sore and bruised all over. Help me get 'er out of the way."

He was badly bitten and his fur coat was in tatters. Blood streamed from a gash in his right temple and there was another in his right cheek. I rubbed his wounds with snow and bandaged them with a piece torn off my once white undershirt.

The next ten minutes were silent. I saw a maze of sharply flickering green pin-points crawling slowly upon us. Indeed, these beasts, who had been man's born companions for more than fifty centuries and had throughout those centuries learned not to fear his fire and his noise, were coming back again with grim hunger a sure incentive. Foot by foot they came, slowly at first, and then more boldly, and in a minute we were battling for life once more. Reaching for a gasoline bomb, I was dragged outside, flat on my back, on the soft, white snow, newly fallen. I had dropped my rifle in the short melee, but luckily still retained my long-bladed pocket knife, the best of weapons for close fighting. I felt the points of strong teeth sing deep into my thighs and shoulders. One big furry fellow growled as he jerked madly at my coat-collar. One time I tore a hairy face loose from my neck and received a severe gash on the back of my hand for my trouble. Three times I felt my knife-blade stick deeply into the soft flesh and I fought that much more terribly, as I heard the accompanying yelps of pain. A dog tore at the heavily booted calf of my left leg and with the other I struck out at him madly and swiftly and arose automatically to my knees. A big dog tore loose my fur cap and his teeth grazed my scalp. A moment later I was aware of a warm trickle covering my face. At the same time my knife sank again and the brute's body fell away from me. Then I was hurled forward into the soft snow, face first, and crouched together at the instant like a battling leopard who is cornered by his foes. I heard Major Cummins shouting when I got to my feet again, took two steps toward the marooned sled, tossing a dog bodily into the air and away from me, felt teeth sink painfully into the fleshy part of my back. Once more I felt the warm ooze of blood; then I was tripped and rolled in the snow again; my head buzzing like a thousand bees. The next moment a huge and ponderous bulk sprawled over me and I heard the major's reassuring voice, soft as a mother's, yet firm as iron, a blade in a velvet sheath. He fired once, kicked a couple of canine enemies from my limp form, and then I became aware of huge arms lifting me into the sally port and the safety of our sled. I heard the heavy slam of the door and the next instant everything became dark, the Stygian ebony void of all consciousness.

"HERE, drink this, Bender," were the first words I heard. "It's molten snow and it's as good as water. I melted it over the gasoline. My God, man, but you are torn up. Lucky for you that you were able to make your way back to the sled as far as you did for I certainly never would have been able to drag you in if you were one foot farther away; and that would have meant the last of both of us. I had to fight the devil himself, as it is; those brutes were savagely hungry. There is not a solitary body left outside, nothing but a few bits of bones and hair and crimson snow."

I opened my eyes and it was daylight. For a moment I felt dizzy but after a drink from the major's proffered cup, full consciousness began to return. I lay on the furs, swathed in crude bandages and red with my own blood. I looked at my companion, the man to whom I owed my life. His mien was stern; a military mask. His shirt and his O. D. breeches were in scarlet-tinted rags, his head was bandaged, and across his left cheek was a still fresh crimson-colored gash, long and deep, showing only too well what those deadly fangs could do. I extended my hand, and I said, "I'll never, never forget this." His answer was a smile.

I had two long scalp wounds and a number of slighter ones. My neck was badly bruised and some skin was torn from my throat and chest. My left arm was somewhat mangled by the sharp teeth of the canine attackers and both of my legs and my back suffered bites.

Noon came and with it came fever. I talked of Clara, mournfully dolefully, with ire. I cursed the major. I shouted and I cried like a peevish child, shrilly and with force. Thrice, so I learned later, the soldier's strong arms pushed me back upon my crude sick-bed of blankets and furs. Once I tore my makeshift bandages from my wounds and ran, semi-naked, out into the snow. The imps of delirium had me in their terrible grip and it was only when complete exhaustion had overtaken me and brought with it an icy sweat, that I became quiet. Cold snow-packs upon my fever-flamed head relieved me a bit and I shut my eyes and drowsed off into a restless sleep, broken by bits of bothersome dreams. I saw the savage, hunger-crazed dogs again and I cried out to my companion to drive them away. They were big dogs, giants, and each of them had the huge, bewhiskered visage of the selfish ex-King of the igloo clan on the hill-top above us. Then came Clara, clad in furs and with a big rifle scattered the dogs to the four quarters of heaven. But the major picked her up in his big arms and carried her away, leaving me behind to the mercies of the mad canine foe. I shouted curses after him as I watched him go. After that I awoke and asked for water. The major handed a tin to me, and I drank greedily, for I was trying to quench a fire within me. Tottering on the fever-ridden brink of that borderland that lies between sleep and consciousness, I shouted to the major to keep off the dogs. Then once again, I opened my eyes. Everything seemed foggy and in the mist stood Clara, the major, tall and portly in his tatters, old Stephen Dunraven wrapped in many furs, and two khaki-clad men, one of them very tall and thin, the other short and stout. As if from a distance and through the dull roar of a pounding surf, I could hear words spoken. Involuntarily I shut my eyes, rubbed them, and then opened them again. Clara, tall and

Junoesque in the olive-drab uniform of a Red Cross ambulance driver, was offering me a drink. Her voice sounded pleasant and I accepted the drink. A white-clad nurse was fixing the bandages on my head with swift, deft fingers that told of much experience. Dunraven was in conversation with the short, fat man who was busy with my lacerated legs. "Not bad, is it, doctor?" he was asking the stout disciple of Aesculapius. The tall man was standing very attentively nearby, a basin in hand. I felt soft, kindly fingers on my wounds and I was indeed a happy man to know that this was reality and not the mad hallucination of a fevered brain. Succor had arrived at last.

An hour later I was prone upon a soft ambulance cot speeding at a mad pace southward through the air. The bulky ex-magnate and man of science was sitting by my side, the medical man was near him, while the major stood at my head. He was relating in a simple way the story of the fight, ungarnished, statistical. Later in the day I learned that soon after my last delirious attack had weakened me and I had fallen into a moaning and a broken slumber, the ever-vigilant soldier, army man that he was, had espied far overhead, outlined like so many tiny, black specks against the leaden sky, a score of northward bound airplanes. Taking them for the searching party, as they actually turned out to be, he hit upon the happy idea of signaling them with fire. Emptying the residue of the contents of the unlucky sled's gasoline tank on some rocks from which he had scraped the snow, he lit this and now that the snow fall had ceased, it flared up and threw a huge column of black smoke toward the heavens. Fifty feet from it the major stood wildly waving his shredded fur coat. One of the pilots, flying lower than the rest and on the lookout for either roving bands of fur-clad Vandals, hungry igloo-dwellers, or wandering survivors of any of the numerous expeditions that had failed to return, had eyes sharp enough to be able to discern the tiny figure and the huge ostrich feather curl of smoke a mile beneath him. He signaled his companions and the rest is history.

It was in the emergency hospital at Washingtonia that the corpulent amateur of science congratulated me. "Bully-boy, Bender," he said, "the major here says that you fought like a wildcat. Lucky, though, that we came in time."

Major Cummins, however, now that the dog war was over, fell from his natural element and became plebian and awkward again. With Clara on his arm, unconscious of my very natural chagrin, he stood at the foot of my cot, looming bulky beside his graceful spouse and recalling to my mind scenes of twenty years ago and schoolboy days, when I had in one class with me a big, overgrown, dull country boy, five grades behind his age.

CHAPTER FOURTEEN
A Retrospect

FIVE swift years have already flown by since the solar system became free of the nebulous frigid ocean in space and since the last of the Sixth Glacier receded beyond the Arctic Circle, and left behind it a barren land; ten years since the first warning cry of Stephen Dunraven, which was echoed so suddenly by the cries of terror from the northern lands. Today I review in retrospect those terrible days when the polar ice fields invaded the temperate zones, safe in the little red brick structure on the brink of the newer New York Bay, the new home the *"Scientific News."* "BIB," sad to say, died about a month ago and now I am the editor. Old Stephen Dunraven was in to see me yesterday. He has grown fatter, grayer, grouchier. Now, however, he is a happy man. Three whole pages, amply illustrated, had I vouchsafed him for the story of the days when the spiders ruled the roost. The big, black cigar that he gave me was delicious, even though I had to be a very patient listener to an arachnidean diatribe that took up the better part of an hour.

Also I learned that the Cordillerian ice sheet of many years ago was nearly five hundred miles wide and extended as far as Washington. As it came swiftly and steadily from the pole, it drove this spider race before its icy fury to seek newer homes in more southern climes, where the Fifth Glacier could never go. Then from the region of the Deewatin Ice Sheet, which, like an immense finger of destruction, reached down from the Hudson Bay countries deep into the heart of the Kansan plains, came another race of spider people, also fugitives from the boreal foe, and they, too, settled at the site of what today is the Mecca of all scientists. There the two races of spiders found the savage ape man, our tree-climbing ancestor, and made of him their hauler of stones and builder of cities. Later came wars, as wars will ever come, where two peoples dwell close to one another. And as the warring arachnideans slaughtered each other, the glacier coming from the north turned the summers into winters and the temperate winters into winters of Arctic climes. Nature, true to its law of destruction of all that is unfit for the place and time, drove the weak spider race ruthlessly into the sand-waste regions with her icy lash from the northern pole. Then the ape man lived wildly, amidst the ruins of old-time grandeur for countless years, in a glory which he never could understand. Time slowly buried them as it passed on beneath its waste of centuries till only the molded tablets remained intact to tell of the history of these strange four-legged people who lived, loved, fought, wrought and died there, and then became one with the darkest oblivion, fugitives, like us, from the northern ice, they who had raised aloft a civilization and were contemporaries of the dawn man, the aurochs, and the giant elk.

In sharp, terse sentences, such an antithesis to his hollow voice, the amateur scientist spoke to me, and every word of his speech sounded like a command from a tomb.

"What strange manners of earthly life," he said, "even now lie buried beneath the soil, since the first bit of animism crawled out of the bathybius ooze at the birth of life, who can say? We, two-legged humankind, are by no means the sole boasters of a rational mind. Only the over-egoed fool dare say he is."

He left a while later, a man who had lost everything, yet faltered not in that which he had chosen as a life work. A rebel forever at odds with the rest of the conservative world, one of the few of its dwellers, who help make progress possible by never crying surrender and by never being satisfied—a skeptic of an old man long ago disillusioned by life, man and pleasures. Yet after his visit, somehow or other, I could not help but think that in reality there had been two Stephen Dunravens. One who had died during the Sixth Ice Age and the other who, sphinxlike, rose out of his shroud, a tender, more contrite man, born of the other's ashes, though he still dared to doubt.

THE great gardener had weeded his earthly garden only too well and left but one-third of its former one and a half billion to refill and recruit the world. Discontent and strife followed fast upon the heels of the settlement of the reclaimed lands. People still insisted upon recalling old boundary lines and their petty hatreds of the past. Men and women wanted power more than they wanted homes. Newer nations sprang up, north, east, south and west, over hill and dale, as soon as the ice had gone and the floods had abated. The first comers, naturally enough, settled upon the choicest of lands and wars soon followed. Then plague followed war as it often does, sparing neither young nor old, and the grim, bony man with the scythe easily settled the disputes that guns had failed to do. For ten years after the Sixth Glacier had joined the hoary past, the heterogeneous population of Europe, and for thrice that long, the more heterogeneous populations of Asia, grappled with itself, while those who had deigned to linger behind in the tropics fought the natives with equal fury.

On this side of the Atlantic, however, things were more quiet. A stricken one-quarter of a once one hundred and twenty-five million came back in four years to a land of many million barren acres. Towns sprang up on prairies and on hills or in vales, and cities along rivers and bays. Farming commenced on the day that the first settler from the south set a rock down on the ground as a stake, and said that these few surrounding acres are to me and mine, home. As I write today, five years after the ice has left, at least for another thousand centuries, the New United States of America that extends from the Rio Grande and the huge Gulf to the icy top of the globe, is starting all over again, just as it did once, nearly five hundred years ago. Cities are springing up over the glacier-demolished terrain, where other cities once had been, on the water-girded site of New York City, on the broad lakefront where once Chicago stood; on San Francisco Bay, on Denver's mile-high altitude. Los Angeles is rebuilding with a furor, just as El Paso, New Orleans and Galveston are doing. The new homes everywhere are mocking the beaten icy foe. By now people only know from memory about the ravages of the Ice King from the poles.

The newcomers are still drifting in, slowly, every day— weary, heartsick men and women from the deserts of Mexico or from the plain lands farther south. Big ships, which had happily survived the big ice walls that for five years unmercifully swept the seven seas, are crossing the oceans back and forth, laden heavily with huge cargoes of food, timber and humanity, while the nucleus of a future railroad system is even now stretching its long fingers of steel into the heart of mountain, desert and plain. Gigantic cargo planes are daily alighting to succor the inhabitants of locations where neither track nor broad highway has penetrated. Wise men, whose eyes could pierce the future's dim veil, are planting tiny trees on the hillsides and lowlands where, only so short a number of years ago, giant trees had stood unbowed. In the turmoil of reconstruction, the nightmare that was the Sixth Glacier is forgotten, and only mourned ones occasionally remind us of those terrible days, when the ice came down from the north and we went wild, yet we can almost forget them as we gaze up out toward the broad horizon and begin again.

Today's morning paper was filled with the spirit of reform. Europe, the five thousand-year-old hot-bed of war and international hatreds, tired of arms and worn by disease, decided to bury the hatchet and start a new world on a better social plan. A protocol was sent out to the rest of the earth's nations. Thus the idealist's dream of a Utopia may after all not be so far away. A catastrophe is sometimes the gift of the gods.

Most of the huge jetties are still standing, though the heating machines have long ago been taken down and put to other uses. Northern Europe and the lower and central parts of our own Atlantic coast are even warmer today than they were during the pre-glacial years. The winters are shorter and less harsh and the summers come early and linger long for the series of small jetties that raise gray, concrete backs out of the blue sea are still at their duty along our coast, pushing the warm equatorial waters of the Gulf Stream toward our shores and I, for one, say, let them stay.

NOW, allow me a bit of time for one more brief bird's-eye view of the world as it is today. The Sixth Glacier has become history already. New York City is made up of islands no more. The sudden rush of the ice fields and the consequent passage for almost five years of a mile thickness of moving ice turned both the Harlem and the East rivers out of their true beds, and now only the bigger Hudson flows into the bay where a newer and greater Statue of Liberty greets it day and night. The once huge metropolis of tall skyscrapers and Brobdingnagian bridges, of avenues of magnificent houses and of more than five million souls, is now the hearth and home of but a mere half-million, a long, drawn-out city facing the open and almost bayless sea. Here and there the faint trace of some street may still show, strange prank of the glacier, and every now and then one does come across some half-buried scrap of steel or masonry which the morning ice field had failed to carry away. The subway alone is the most intact, and although caved-in at scores of places and full of debris of all kinds, it still is the New York subway of ten years ago and New Yorkers daily look forward to the time when they shall be able to use it again. One mile of ice stood over it for four long years, but it had borne the burden nobly.

Both Japan and Britain had been pushed out of their sites by the glacier while little Iceland had been torn in halves and shot two hundred miles to the south. The Isle of Man is no more. When the Sixth Glacier retreated, it was no longer there. In the Antarctic part of the world, the glacier had been more merciful, probably because there was not so much to ruin. The ghosts of Capetown, Kimberly, Melbourne and of Sydney are today looking down from some municipal Paradise in the skies, upon the newer cities that have taken their earthly places. Sahara is a sea, one with the cerulean Mediterranean. Gobi is a lake.

Our own southern states, unfortunate victims of crazed mobs from the north, are once more breathing normally, and under the strain of the added millions, are living anew. Many of Cuba's newest population have refused to return to the states. They seem to like that hot little island, whose population today is thirty million.

But from Asia came uglier news. The yellow men from the north have decided to stay south of the Himalayas. China, consequently is barren and the Russ is pouring into its fertile southern parts. Japan retrogressed in civilization's scale for almost a thousand years, a tiny island kingdom full of hills and flowers, which proved so terrible a death-trap to its fifty millions. Now about one million little swarthy men and women live quiet bucolic lives in a barren, mountain land that was once opulent with pretty outlandish houses and blossoming cherry trees.

The Alps in Europe and the Rockies and the Sierra Nevadas here have caught in their grips and have refused to let go here and there a piece of the glacier as it went back. Now in many a crevice and gorge flow slowly down to the plain below, huge glaciers, offspring of a huger one, prodigals who would never return.

YESTERDAY was Christmas Day and the world forgot and made merry. In the new Paris, a little, unpaved city on the Seine, there was exhibited a relic picked up near the Moroccan city of Fez by a Moorish donkey-driver, a piece of the tall Eifel tower that had been carried across the wide Mediterranean by the moving ice, a mute witness of the pomp and glamour that once had been Paris. A week ago a farmer in Virginia unearthed the huge pyramid top-piece of the Washington Monument. One hundred thousand years from now, when the time will be ripe for the Seventh Glacier and the northern world will have to hurry south again, maybe some future Stephen Dunraven will pick up a piece of the Brooklyn Bridge or the White House and warn a sleepy world of the coming of the ice.

Just one more little picture ere I close. Clara, plumper now and quite matronly, and the Major, now an army man no more, comes to see me often. They, too, have settled in the new city of New York that stands facing the sea. Her father, still a bit grouchy and full of gout, is with them—the proud grandpa of two long-legged boys—still the same old pessimist nevertheless. He talks spiders with me, whenever we meet, sometimes, perhaps, glaciers, but never has he yet mentioned the many lost millions or the miles of car lines that were once upon a time his and were stolen by the ice. Old Hillsboro is still alive and happy over the fact that the glacier allowed his journal to survive. I myself am a confirmed bachelor with a dog and a pipe. Cummins is once more out of his element, an unsuccessful realtor, who tried hard but in vain to interest me in Jersey lots and is forever telling prospective customers of those hectic days when the polar regions came south on an errand of destruction, to which I, too, have devoted some earlier words.

THE END

If you've enjoyed this book, you will not want to miss these terrific titles…

ARMCHAIR SCI-FI & HORROR DOUBLE NOVELS, $12.95 each

D-131   **COSMIC KILL** by Robert Silverberg
BEYOND THE END OF SPACE by John W. Campbell

D-132   **THE DARK OTHER** by Stanley Weinbaum)
WITCH OF THE DEMON SEAS by Poul Anderson

D-133   **PLANET OF THE SMALL MEN** by Murray Leinster
MASTERS OF SPACE by E. E. "Doc" Smith & E. Everett Evans

D-134   **BEFORE THE ASTEROIDS** by Harl Vincent
SIXTH GLACIER, THE by Marius

D-135   **AFTER WORLD'S END** by Jack Williamson
THE FLOATING ROBOT by David Wright O'Brien

D-136   **NINE WORLDS WEST** by Paul W. Fairman
FRONTIERS BEYOND THE SUN by Rog Phillips

D-137   **THE COSMIC KINGS** by Edmond Hamilton
LONE STAR PLANET by H. Beam Piper & John J. McGuire

D-138   **BEYOND THE DARKNESS** by S. J. Byrne
THE FIRELESS AGE by David H. Keller, M. D.

D-139   **FLAME JEWEL OF THE ANCIENTS** by Edwin L. Graber
THE PIRATE PLANET by Charles W. Diffin

D-140   **ADDRESS: CENTAURI** by F. L. Wallace
IF THESE BE GODS by Algis Budrys

ARMCHAIR SCIENCE FICTION & HORROR CLASSICS, $12.95 each

C-58   **THE WITCHING NIGHT**
by Leslie Waller

C-59   **SEARCH THE SKY**
by Frederick Pohl and C. M. Kornbluth

C-60   **INTRIGUE ON THE UPPER LEVEL**
by Thomas Tempel Hoyne

ARMCHAIR SCI-FI & HORROR GEMS SERIES, $12.95 each

G-15   **SCIENCE FICTION GEMS, Vol. Eight**
Keith Laumer and others

G-16   **HORROR GEMS, Vol. Eight**
Algernon Blackwood and others